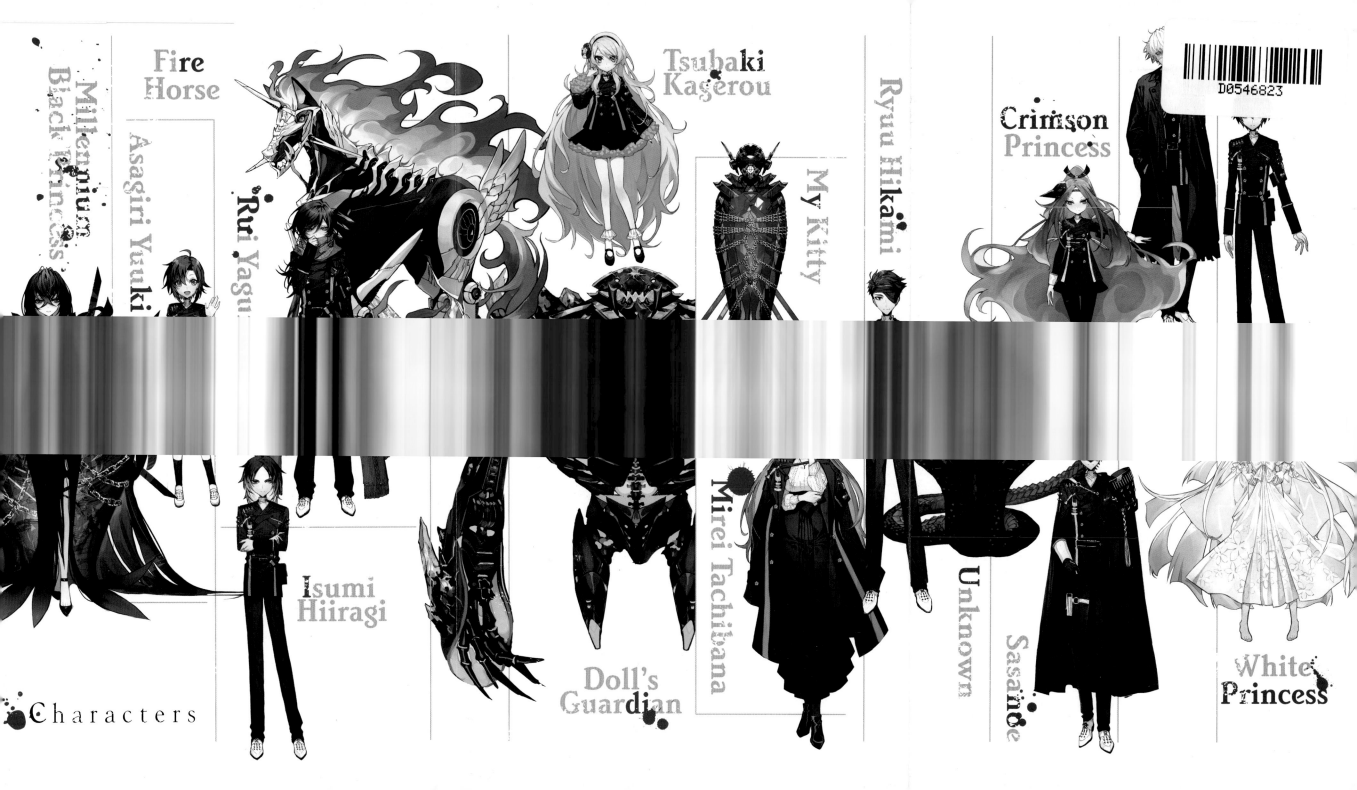

Millennium
Black Princess

Asagiri Yuuki

Fire
Horse

Rui Yasu

Tsubaki
Kagerou

My Kitty

Ryuu Hikami

Crimson
Princess

D0546823

Isumi
Hiiragi

Doll's
Guardian

Mirei Tachibana

Unknown

Sasante

White
Princess

Characters

"Death is not something we invite, but only **death** or **victory** awaits us at the end of the **fight**."

THE 3RIDE OF DEMISE

Keishi Ayasato

Illustration by
murakaruki

YEN
ON

New York

THE BRIDE OF DEMISE

KEISHI AYASATO

Translation by Jordan Taylor
Cover art by murakaruki

This book is a work of fiction. Names, characters, places, and incidents are the product of the author's imagination or are used fictitiously. Any resemblance to actual events, locales, or persons, living or dead, is coincidental.

SHUEN NO HANAYOME Vol.1
©Keishi Ayasato 2020
First published in Japan in 2020 by KADOKAWA CORPORATION, Tokyo.
English translation rights arranged with KADOKAWA CORPORATION, Tokyo, through TUTTLE-MORI AGENCY, INC., Tokyo.
English translation © 2022 by Yen Press, LLC

Yen On
150 West 30th Street, 19th Floor
New York, NY 10001

Visit us at yenpress.com • facebook.com/yenpress • twitter.com/yenpress
yenpress.tumblr.com • instagram.com/yenpress

First Yen On Edition: August 2022
Edited by Yen On Editorial: Emma McClain, Rachel Mimms
Designed by Yen Press Design: Andy Swist

Yen On is an imprint of Yen Press, LLC.
The Yen On name and logo are trademarks of Yen Press, LLC.

The publisher is not responsible for websites (or their content) that are not owned by the publisher.

Library of Congress Cataloging-in-Publication Data
Names: Ayasato, Keishi, author. | Mura, Karuki, illustrator. | Taylor, Jordan (Translator), translator.
Title: The bride of demise / Keishi Ayasato ; illustration by murakaruki ; translation by Jordan Taylor.
Other titles: Shuen no hanayome. English
Description: New York, NY : Yen On, 2022.
Identifiers: LCCN 2022010509 | ISBN 9781975337940 (v. 1 ; trade paperback) | ISBN 9781975337964 (v. 2 ; trade paperback) | ISBN 9781975338015 (v. 3 ; trade paperback)
Subjects: LCGFT: Fantasy fiction. | Light novels.
Classification: LCC PL867.5.Y36 S4813 2022 | DDC 895.63/6—dc23/eng/20220311
LC record available at https://lccn.loc.gov/2022010509

ISBNs: 978-1-9753-3794-0 (paperback)
978-1-9753-3795-7 (ebook)

10 9 8 7 6 5 4 3 2 1

LSC-C

Printed in the United States of America

Cover and illustrations by murakaruki

Kou Kaguro opened his violet eyes.

…Kou stared in blank amazement at what he saw.

Around him were mechanical devices embedded in thick vegetation, but he lacked the knowledge to determine what they were.

This place had originally been a dome resembling a birdcage. The structure was highly decorative, made as it was from a frame of unknown black metal and reinforced glass. At the center was a strange glass case, still intact, that resembled a casket.

A girl sat up from inside the case. Her lips were stained red from Kou Kaguro's blood—blood that had showered the area when he'd fallen.

She slowly swallowed it.

Wings burst from her back. The wings were strange and mechanical and didn't match her white skin. They tore through her flesh and unfurled, filling the area around her. There was a flash of blue light and a harsh, grating sound of machinery operating. The wicked metal parts glittered. But then the wings folded away in the blink of an eye, completely gone, and returned to her body as if they'd never been there.

She slowly blinked, then looked toward Kou.

Her blue eyes were like the sky, her white hair like the snow.

Her arms and legs were graceful, and the slender yet tempered build of her body brought to mind a steel sword.

The beautiful girl stretched out her hand. Kou instinctively moved his arm in response. Intense pain shot through his entire body, but he forced his hand up. She was still too far.

Seeing this, she blinked. She severed the cables connected to her body and walked forward. When she reached Kou, she took his hand and reopened her mechanical wings.

The surrounding vegetation was slashed and torn. Millions of petals fluttered about. White flowers, nearly silver, flitted through the air.

They momentarily froze before plummeting to the ground.

Amid this hallowed scene, the girl took a knee.

She pressed her lips to Kou's fingers.

"From this moment on, you are my master. My wings belong to you. I am delighted to meet you, my beloved. And oh, how I have waited for you. My name is White Princess. My alias is Curtain Call."

Just like a knight of legend, like a princess in a fairy tale, the awoken girl made an oath.

"Though you may become broken, beaten, or lost, I shall be by your side for all eternity."

In that moment, he wed the end of the world.

It was a story from long, long, oh so long ago.

Someone's face entered his blurred vision.

Just then, a single tear ran down his cheek.

"…Huh, that's weird."

With a tilt of his head, he reached a hand up to his eye. Kou didn't usually cry. In fact, he couldn't remember ever crying, no matter how sad something was. But now he couldn't stop.

He was baffled by the tears that flowed without reason. Before him, a girl with vaguely childlike features similarly tilted her head in confusion.

"Hmm? Kou, are you crying? Why?"

"I'm not sure… Maybe I had a bad dream?"

"I don't think I've ever seen you cry. I wonder what you were dreaming about," she said, mystified. She blinked. Her large chestnut-colored eyes complemented her short brown hair.

Kou took in her full form. She wore a vermilion uniform and hugged a textbook and several research books to her chest.

He recalled what he knew about her.

She was Asagiri Yuuki, a girl in the same year as him. He also reflected on some important and obvious facts.

Kou Kaguro is a student who lives at the Twilight Academy, a boarding school of magic, he thought.

And suddenly those thoughts turned back to the day of the entrance ceremony.

There was a particular reason why it was difficult to describe starting school at the Twilight Academy as pleasant. During the ceremony, many of the new students were trembling with nervousness or even crying. Lined neatly in their rows, they were engulfed in despair and confusion.

Kou was the only one who wasn't bothered.

After the strict and austere ceremony, he made his way to the buildings that housed their classes. Each major had separate dorms and classrooms located in buildings scattered across the vast complex. The wings of the Central Headquarters building stretched to the east and west, like a gallant bird. Its majestic presence, too, seemed to overwhelm many of the students.

But Kou wasn't particularly affected by it; he just kept walking. That's when someone suddenly called out to him.

"You're not afraid, are you? I'm jealous."

Kou turned back. There was a petite girl standing right beside him.

He looked into her eyes and saw she was frightened. And that's why he answered her.

"No, I'm not afraid. I don't mind joining you, if it'll make you feel better."

He held out his hand to her. She blinked as she took it and said, *"You're sweet."*

"I just thought it'd be nice if I could help a bit. I don't think that counts as being sweet," replied Kou, and the girl smiled. Then she told him her name.

"I'm Asagiri. Asagiri Yuuki."

The two of them had been friends ever since.

Kou confirmed all that information, then asked, "Asagiri, was I... sleeping?"

Asagiri's eyes widened, then a gentle smile spread across her face.

"You're still pretty out of it, aren't you, Kou? You just said yourself you probably had a bad dream. And can't you tell if you were sleeping?"

"I don't know if that's necessarily true. Right now, I can't tell... Actually, you're right, I'm definitely spacing."

He turned his head from side to side. He felt like the remains of the strange dream were still stuck to his eyeballs.

He rubbed his eyes, then looked around. He was in a large room. The windows on all four walls were hidden behind closed black curtains.

... the scarlet carpet were rows of chairs facing the center of

stude...

Architecture, among o...

Academic study was considered necessa... it was specialized toward one particular goal.

Kou suddenly dropped his gaze. There was a messy scrawl written in his notebook.

History can be divided into two major periods:
Before the Kihei appeared and after.

"You just get fed up hearing about it so much, don't you? I know I'm sick of it," said Asagiri with a sigh.

"Yeah, I can't say it's interesting to hear about something you already memorized over and over again." When Kou agreed with her, Asagiri nodded deeply.

"Right? It's got to be pretty bad if even you're sick of it."

"I wouldn't say I'm sick of it. Not yet."

"Oh, come on, Kou. You're too laid-back."

Asagiri stuck out her tongue, then touched the paper with a slender finger. The sentences describing the fundamentals' class lesson were frightening, yet Asagiri smiled for some reason as she traced over Kou's messy handwriting.

Though he was confused, he cast his gaze ahead.

In the center of the lecture hall was a massive floating panel made from magic crystal. The 3D projection used in the class that had just ended was still being formed inside the thick crystal.

It displayed a strange, terrifying form. Outwardly, it appeared hard. Yet at the same time, it had a lifelike viciousness to it. It was both organic and inorganic. It was like an insect yet also like a beast. And at the same time, it wasn't like either.

They were strange beings, an amalgamation of beast and machine.

Kou's eyes narrowed as he confirmed what it was.

...It's a Type B kihei.

The word *kihei* could be written with the characters for *demon* and *soldier*. Or it could be written with the characters for *machine* and *soldier*. Either one was fine.

All they did was attack humans. They didn't eat humans; they just killed them.

Put simply, they were humanity's enemy.

Kou thought back to the lecture on the kihei.

Before Erosion... Imperial Year 25 BE.

The kihei abruptly appeared and attacked the empire, throwing humanity into chaos. Sixty percent of the population at the time was killed. Countless kihei invaded imperial territory. Contact with other countries was cut off, leaving the empire isolated. Ever since, they had been forced to fight a long and grueling war on their own.

That's all in the distant past.

Those "other countries" that used to exist had long ago faded from memory. The empire's independent magic research allowed the country to build impenetrable defenses, which, in turn, had led to the modicum of peace enjoyed today.

This academy was also part of those plans.

Large numbers of pupils gathered in these houses of learning.

All of them, including Kou Kaguro, were official students.

Not just students but soldiers, too. They studied and also served as the empire's infantry.

The students existed for the purpose of fighting the kihei.

But...

At this point, Kou focused his thoughts back on the present.

The polished wooden chairs of the lecture hall were arranged in row after row. On the ceiling was a wavering fire spell, contained within complex and conjoined silvery cages. Beside Kou stood Asagiri, her research books pressed tight against her chest.

At a glance, there were no signs of the terrifying war to be seen in daily life at the Academy.

There was probably no point in dwelling on the current state of things.

"Right... I should probably get going, too."

Kou quickly put his textbook into his satchel. Holding it at his side, ...d to catch up and walk beside

close to the beginning as possible,

Kou didn't have any particular interest in the ceremony practice, but Asagiri seemed like she wanted to see it. In which case, he should join her. His mind made up, he started walking faster.

Asagiri clenched a fist and nodded in accomplishment. Though a bit confused, Kou nodded back.

He didn't know why she did that, but it was good that she was happy.

Sometimes Asagiri could be a bit childlike. And Kou had always felt protective of her for some reason. Why was that? Kou felt like he'd known someone long ago... Someone who had occasionally acted childlike.

I still have no idea who that person is, though.

Kou felt a strange emptiness. A void grew in his chest, something resembling an aching loneliness. But he shook his head and kept walking.

There was no way he could fill that void right now.

The two of them walked across the scarlet carpet and, on their way out, found a student who hadn't left his seat.

He was glaring at the figure still displayed in the magic crystal.

Kou approached him from behind. Asagiri whispered for Kou to stop, but this student had an aura about him that Kou found difficult to ignore. Kou placed a hand on his shoulder.

In as calm a tone as he could manage, Kou said, "Isumi, time to go back to Research. You shouldn't dwell on this—"

"Shut up! A white mask like you just doesn't get it!"

The student threw an Academy-specific insult back at Kou. He brushed aside Kou's hand, which then hovered pointlessly in the air.

Masks had a special significance in this academy. During ceremonies, people wore masks with all sorts of patterns, like foxes and cats. They imitated masks used in the empire's festivals. A white mask, then, referred to a mask before it had been altered.

It was smooth, with no color or embellishment, nothing more than a white surface.

It represented neither an animal nor a person but something unfamiliar and suspicious.

In other words, Isumi was calling Kou suspicious, someone who showed no emotions or expressions.

Kou nodded in acceptance. There was some logic to that; Kou did have fewer emotional ups and downs compared to your average person. Asagiri might call it spacey, while Isumi might call it suspicious. The majority was probably on Isumi's side. But it made Asagiri angry.

Like a cat whose tail had just been stepped on, she raised her voice.

"That's mean, Isumi! Kou's not a white mask! If you hate the kihei that much, you should have chosen the Combat course, not Research!"

"I don't want to hear it from someone who made the same decision I did, Asagiri. And everyone calls Kou a white mask. A lucky bastard like him… He can't even understand why I'm angry at the kihei, why I hate them, but he still butts in!"

"Why are you always so unpleasant? I might understand if Kou were a Coexister. It sucks to hear someone be like, 'We should make peace with the kihei' and all. But Kou's not one of them, so I don't get what you're so upset about."

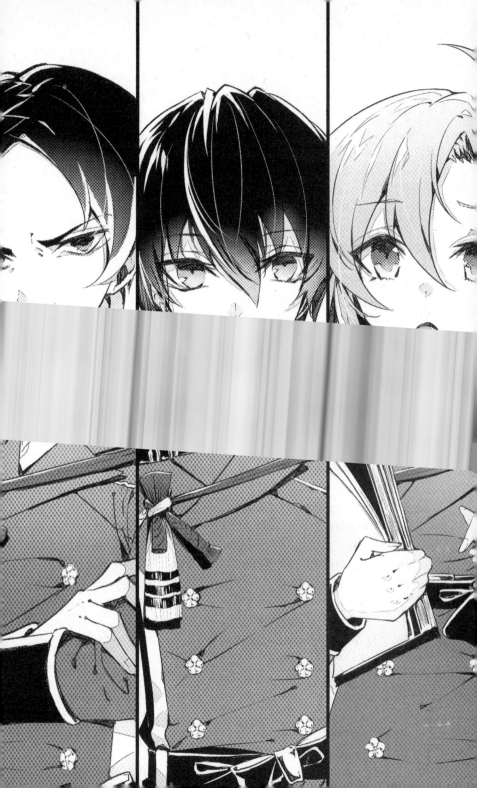

"You're right, he's not a Coexister nutjob…but he's never lost a family member to the kihei! He's fundamentally different from us. Someone as carefree as him shouldn't go running his mouth…"

"Well, my parents are dead, too," said Kou honestly, without thinking. It was incredible how cold the air seemed to get. Kou had only meant to say something relevant to the current conversation, so he didn't understand this reaction. His eyes darted back and forth; he felt somewhat uncomfortable.

Kou, Isumi, and Asagiri were orphans. Seventy percent of the children housed in the Academy were. Out of that 70 percent, 90 percent of them lost their family to the kihei. Kou's situation was different, though.

His parents were killed by human hands.

Kou was without any memories of his early childhood. Every time he tried thinking back to that time in his life, he was assailed by a severe headache. It was possible he was subconsciously refusing to remember because the death of his parents had been so horrifying. Once he'd come to that conclusion, he gave up and stopped trying.

No one had even told him the details of what happened. All he knew was that a burglar had murdered his parents.

Without any other family to rely on, Kou had ended up here.

Orphans of the empire were guaranteed food, clothing, and shelter. In return, they were all sent to the Academy and either fought as students or were employed to maintain the facility. Even so, many of the students who managed to survive past their graduation set up homes in the segregated defense zone in front of the imperial capital. Their children were also required to enroll at the Academy. Nevertheless, the goal of many students was to earn citizenship in the segregated defense zone.

Revenge against the kihei, among other reasons, led a second group to remain at the Academy. Along with their families, they lent the place the feeling of a small country.

In general, it appeared peaceful inside the Academy's walls.

But each and every one of their lives was still in a certain amount of danger.

That's why so many of the students were shaking with nerves on that first day. A lot of them were crying, too. I think I was the only one who stayed calm… Everyone seems to have gotten used to it by now, though, even comfortable with it. But Isumi has me a bit worried… I wish I could help somehow.

Unlike Kou, who was lost in thought, Isumi seemed shaken for some reason. In a quiet voice, he muttered, "Sorry." Before Kou could say anything back, Isumi violently grabbed his bag and rushed off. Asagiri's shoulders slumped.

"Hah… He's not a bad guy at heart," she said.

"You're right; he's not… Should we go?" asked Kou.

"Yeah."

The two walked through the lecture hall.

From outside came the splendid sound of the Music Corps

Magic was used to its fullest for the performance danced gracefully through the air in time with the music.

Many students were in the area, cheering.

Kou noticed someone he recognized. Some girls from the Department of Magic Research were among the crowd watching the show. One of them turned their way, her blond tied-back hair waving as she did. She was a friend of Asagiri's.

The girl saw Kou and Asagiri and beamed. She slipped from the crowd and came over to Asagiri.

"Good for you, Asagiri! To be honest, I'm not sure about your taste, but… I see you invited Kou. Looks like my advice is working out for you!"

"Forget about that! Focus on the march; it's incredible!"

Asagiri turned bright red and pushed her friend's back. As they made their way forward, Asagiri called out, "Kou, wait here a sec; I'll be right back!"

"Yeah, I'll be here…," said Kou. He smiled slightly as he watched them leave and said, "They look like good friends."

That's when he saw it. In the direction of the girls, far in the distance, was an oddly organic wall. He couldn't help narrowing his eyes against its foul appearance. Its complex structure looked like it had been made from a fusion of beasts of all types and sizes. Countless mechanical wings and legs formed the automatic attack system of the sophisticated magic wall.

Kou had heard it was a relic from long before the Erosion Period, before history was recorded.

The Academy was surrounded by it. An even more powerful magic wall apparently towered over the imperial capital. But it still wasn't enough to protect the entire country. The slums running along the periphery of the simple city walls were particularly vulnerable.

There were also many people who temporarily left the empire to make money in the ruins. Children were constantly losing their families that way.

While the students did have required military service, there was no risk of a surprise attack from the kihei in the Academy. So one could say it was relatively peaceful.

…Minus that one exception, thought Kou as his gaze left the wall.

Some students were relaxing at a café, while others were going to the bookstore or armory. Students were allowed to upgrade their equipment at their own discretion. A group of female students was engaged in lively conversation as they cut up slices of cake made from spirit-synthesized food. Not even the Academy had the resources necessary to provide everyone with natural food. The people who lived here knew nothing but the taste of synthesized food, but that didn't mean the standards of living here were low.

The carefree performance of the Music Corps was proof enough of that, with its brass instruments pointed high into the air.

There was a burst of petals, made from magic, causing a gold wave that rushed into the sky and faded. The crowd applauded. Above them, pink and aqua petals danced chaotically through the air before melting into the wind.

A momentary silence fell over the crowd as they waited for the next performance. That's when Asagiri came back. Her breath was ragged, like she'd been arguing with her friend.

"Sorry for the wait. L-let's go, Kou!" she said.

"Looks like there's going to be more, though. You don't want to see the rest? You're already here. I don't mind if you want to go back to your friends."

"It's fine! I'll go with you! If you're going, I'll go, too!"

"Really? All right, then let's go together."

Kou gave a sideways glance at the parade, then moved toward the Research buildings with Asagiri. The students had separate buildings for classes and their dorms, determined by their major.

... of Magic Research buildings, which were for Kou

... calming navy. For just a moment

... the same color as

Meanwhile, ...

were perfect. And Central ... class students were allowed to enter it. The ... single teleportation device that led to the imperial capital, as well ... collection of equipment from the best of the best of each type of magic. The building itself was dazzling, too, with a facade that resembled a castle. However, it was said that first-class students were limited to those under the direct command of Kagura, the most powerful teacher.

Trying to join that group was way too ambitious. Kou didn't even have any real complaints about life in the Department of Magic Research.

"I don't think the beds are even that hard," he said.

"Um, Kou, what are you talking about? The Research beds are hard as rocks," said Asagiri.

"Really? Maybe I'm just used to them."

"You totally are! Ah, I want to hurry up and get my special qualification. If I help a lot with research, then I can save up money until I can buy a different bed, and even…"

"You want a phantom beast, don't you?"

"Yes! I want to research phantom beasts and minerals from the ruins," replied Asagiri energetically. Those students who completed their course and combat training could then receive a certain qualification. At that point, they were provided with a stipend, the amount of which was determined by their contribution to research or battle missions.

For some time, Asagiri had been looking forward to purchasing and raising her own phantom beast.

In general, students were free to choose which department they joined. At a glance, the Academy appeared peaceful.

But Kou Kaguro knew better.

Students who choose the Department of Combat have a strong thirst for revenge against the kihei.

Either that or they needed money. Or maybe they wanted priority rights to live in the segregated defense zone. And 80 percent of the military was made up of students, with the other 20 percent regular soldiers. And 40 percent of the total would die in routine battles.

And when there's an exception...

Asagiri sensed the sorrow in Kou's violet eyes.

Beside him, her small frame bounced up and down.

"You know, we've also got to go gather stuff for research."

"Yeah, that's right. Seems like everyone's getting used to it by now and working together well," said Kou, trying to reassure her.

Asagiri's shoulders relaxed, but a fleeting smile crossed her face. She laced her fingers together and stiffly said, "I want to help the fight against the kihei from behind, at least. That's why I chose Research. I don't regret that decision, but...I'm always praying that the worst-case scenario doesn't happen. Not just for myself, but for you, too, Kou. I pray that we are never put in danger."

"Thanks, Asagiri. But...what kind of danger are you thinking of?"

"Well, like, running into a Type A or a Special Type, and we're all killed..."

Kou Kaguro's vision twisted and swirled.

Everything went black, as if a curtain dropped before his eyes.

His surroundings began to shift.

The change happened so quickly, like someone flipping through the pages of a book they were bored of rereading.

* * *

"Kou, are you awake?"

Kou Kaguro opened his violet eyes.

Asagiri's call echoed deep in his mind.

His vision was filled with green.

In front of him was a window made from very pure magic crystal.

Some sort of ivy-like plant swayed on the other side. He couldn't feel the flow of air, though, wearing full magic armor as he was. He was having difficulty breathing and tried to rub his eyes, then realized his hands couldn't directly touch his face through the armor. He gave up

They were currently on the outside on a mission to do research. The armor covering his body and the overflowing vegetation were proof of that. There was no way he could fall asleep. But he did certainly have a strange break in his consciousness.

If felt as if he'd had an incredibly long dream.

A long, long, nostalgic dream.

"Is that so? You took a long time to reply, though, if you really were awake…"

"He probably just dozed off. Not like a white mask's got any sense of fear, after all."

"Drop it already, Isumi!"

"Come on, stop fighting. There's no point questioning him. Yeah, you've got some balls if you managed to fall asleep on the outside, but… Even if you're awake, Kou, you need to focus, yeah? Let's hurry up and get this over with. We could end up dead if we screw this up… Not that I think we'll see the worst-case scenario."

"Understood. I'm sorry."

Kou responded plainly to the upperclassman's admonishment following Asagiri and Isumi's bickering.

Magic crystals delivered the others' messages directly into their ears while eliminating background noise and the sound and vibrations of their armor moving. If Kou focused solely on the sounds coming to him, he could almost be tricked into thinking they were chatting back in a peaceful classroom. But that wasn't what was really happening. They were in a place of death, and everyone knew it.

At the same time, Kou understood that wasn't the case.

They were currently walking through the remains of a building from the prehistoric period. Areas like this were the birthplace of magic technology development. Yet they were also the enigmatic root of the current situation. These ruins dotted imperial territory from before the Erosion Period.

The people of the empire would take objects from the ruins to conduct research and develop magic technology. But one day, kihei flooded out from every site.

The kihei attacked humans, slaughtering them without end or reason.

And that marked the beginning of a long history of war.

They still hadn't solved all the mysteries of the ruins, and they still hadn't figured out just how many kihei there were in total. However, the Department of Exploration had focused on creating safe routes in a number of the ruins. These areas had been completely cleared of incubation nests as well as live kihei and were designated as Clean Zones. Kou and the others were currently in one of those zones.

Not long ago, those kihei that appeared had been eliminated by the Department of Combat. It was practically unheard of for new kihei to appear in a Clean Zone that had just been cleared out.

Which was one reason why no one from the ever-busy Combat Department accompanied them. Everyone present was from the Department of Magic Research.

"All right then, let's go. Don't fall too far behind."

"Understood. I won't stop no matter what happens," said Kou.

"Let's just hope nothing does happen," replied the upperclassman over the comms in a cheery voice.

Kou looked forward. Nearby were the skeletal remains of structures made from as-of-yet-unknown materials. Plants spread their sturdy roots across them, bringing a serenity to the scene. Sometimes they would even see a small animal. Looking ahead, Kou could see his comrades walking in a straight line.

Every one of them was enveloped in the matte black of the magic armor.

It looked like their forms had been cut out from the dark of night. It actually seemed kind of ridiculous, considering the armor's complete lack of camouflage. They couldn't change its color, though, due to the ... them look like black knights out of a fairy tale. Per- ... to call it armor.

... ...ntions to come out of the

best ... kihei. The problem w... didn't understand the fundamenta... it was still shrouded in mystery.

In order to make magic armor, they used body parts from kihei.

The researchers had merely felt out how it worked through trial and error. By no means had they unraveled the mysteries of the kihei. And there was another important point:

You can only fight a Type B kihei in magic armor.

If you happened to run into a Type A or a Special Type, both more powerful than Type B, then you were better off dead. However, an average student could take on a Type B kihei, and students with a bit of battle experience could take on several. The basic parts of magic armor could be duplicated with material from an incubation nest. But in order to maintain development, they had to have fresh kihei corpses.

They needed the enemy in order to fight the enemy.

It was quite the paradox.

But research couldn't advance without materials.

That's why Kou and the others from Research were out trying to recover Type B corpses.

"*I see it; there it is,*" said the third-year student. Kou narrowed his violet eyes.

Then his vision suddenly opened up. He'd stepped into a wide-open circular space. The roof that likely existed long ago had been blown off, leaving pillars here and there. Short grass grew over the ground.

It was there, in the center.

Kou focused his attention on the strange mass.

He was used to seeing them, this thing that was lying on the ground, yet something still felt wrong about them every time.

It was both organic and inorganic. It was like an insect yet also like a beast. The one in front of them now looked a bit like a spider. Neither its eight legs nor its red glass eyes looked like they would start moving again.

Kou calmly confirmed the information they'd received from the Exploration Squad that had been through before.

...It's a Type B kihei.

Here was one of the students' enemies.

And they started to dismember it.

* * *

The upperclassmen got to work, their motions efficient.

With practiced ease, they proceeded with the dismemberment.

Fire magic was used to heat blades to extreme temperatures. Those blades, along with the strong grip of the magic armor, allowed them to sever each of the kihei's joints, then slice the body into pieces that could be carried.

Kou and the other underclassmen didn't even need to help. It was all over in less than thirty minutes.

The underclassmen formed a line to take turns picking up fragments of the kihei. When it came to Kou's turn, the upperclassman in charge lifted a particularly large chunk. It seemed he'd heard the exchange from earlier.

"*You can have this one, since you started spacing out.*"

"Fine, I guess. Seems a bit unreasonable, though," replied Kou.

He held out his arms despite his complaints, and the upperclassman placed a massive claw across them. Kou felt a heavy impact, even through the magic armor. The fifth-year upperclassman seemed to chuckle. He looked around, then gave his signal.

"Good, everyone's got a piece. Let's get this show on—"

A split second later, his head was gone.

His neck had been severed, right through the armor.

The head flew in a clean arc through the air, then bounced and rolled across the ground.

Seconds later, an absurd amount of blood fountained skyward.

The headless body spun slowly around, then collapsed.

There were a few seconds of silence. A moment later, an explosion of screams broke out. One after another, violent shrieks twisted into a

He ran through his memories.

A moment earlier, a translucent membrane flickered out from the shadow of a pillar. It was softer than a flower petal and sharper than a blade. The shimmering sheet resembled a veil. That veil enveloped a humanlike figure that walked smoothly across the floor.

Kou forced down his desire to deny what he saw. There was no point running from the truth.

He released his breath and reopened his comms.

"Sighting confirmed. It's a Special Type."

As he said that, Kou understood. They had won the bad luck lottery. This was that "worst-case scenario." When efficiency was prioritized, death could smile upon you at any time. So many people had encountered this before.

That's why they already knew the answer.

Regular students couldn't win against a Special Type, not even if there were a hundred of them.

Everyone in the squad was going to die.

No one here was going to make it home alive.

* * *

Knives flashed, guns fired, all in vain.

The gun set on the magic armor's shoulder gave directionality to the user's magic. Lightning shot out of the end with high accuracy. The Special Type kihei stiffened for a moment, but it wasn't even enough to slow its approach.

A few sets of magic armor, and the people inside them, were gently caressed by the membrane. It was such a gentle motion, like it was stroking their skin.

The armor briefly slipped apart from itself. Gallons of blood burst out.

Plants were dyed red; people's screams filled the area.

If students from Combat had been here, they would have been able to come up with an appropriate response, though that wouldn't change the outcome. Kou knew. Ten or so skilled fighters would make a battle strategy, they'd lose most of them, and they may or may not be able to destroy the kihei. It was more likely they'd all die, the same as Kou and the others were about to.

It was a Special Type, a kihei particularly powerful in battle. There were very few people who could run into that and come out alive.

Yet Kou did remember a rumor he'd heard. It was about a teacher at the Academy famous for being the most powerful: Kagura. His Elite Squad alongside him might be able to win. But even if he prayed for their help, no one was coming.

"*Hurry, hurry, send a distress— Gah!*"

"*This can't be happening! No, no, nooooooo! Gck!*"

Heart-wrenching death screams were delivered to Kou with vivid clarity. Then an overwhelming silence gaped open, like a hole.

The killing continued; the panic didn't end.

If things carried on as they were, every single one of them would end up dead.

Not even the upperclassmen could give advice at a time like this. Out of the sea of many screams, Kou picked out two specific voices.

"No...no...no! Not here; I don't want to die; I haven't even accomplished anything!"

"Shit, shit shit shit! Not me, not me!"

Asagiri's and Isumi's cries assaulted Kou's ears.

A strong feeling came over him. He loathed seeing people die before his eyes. It was too much.

He could no longer endure the feeling of his own helplessness.

Blood, bone, flesh, corpses, flames, tears.

Someone looking so incredibly sad.

...time flashed before his eyes.

...He fumbled, groped through all

"I'll draw ...

can!"

"Kou? You can't do that!"

"Don't be a moron! I don't want something like that from you!"

"Isumi, take Asagiri with you. I'm counting on you!" shouted Kou, setting his volume to as loud as he could. He then cut off his comms.

Just then, he had the feeling Asagiri and Isumi said something. But he didn't hear it.

He had no intention of listening to their words, their efforts to stop him, their heartfelt cries.

Many of the students hated the kihei and wanted to kill them. When faced with this unfairness, they might rise up. But Kou was sure no one would follow him.

Most of the students in the Department of Magic Research were cowards. They all wanted to live. And Kou wasn't a well-liked person. He had his concerns about Asagiri, but Isumi wasn't the sort to betray a final request.

Kou prepared himself and turned to face the Special Type.

It was simply toying with its prey.

Its shimmering membrane fluttered gracefully as it tossed the severed head, still in its helmet. It caught the head, then tossed it again. Then it suddenly sliced the head into four parts. The black helmet split, its contents turned into a shower of cerebral fluid.

Kou thrust a sword down by the kihei's feet, pinning the membrane into the ground.

It stopped moving for a brief moment.

Before it could pull the sword out, Kou lined up a shot and fired lightning magic at the blade.

Electricity ran through the kihei, and it spasmed violently. In that moment, Kou opened his comms again.

"Scatter!"

Like tiny spiders running out from their mother, the crowd of students dashed away. One small-framed student briefly tried to run toward Kou, but another one grabbed them and dragged them away. That was probably Asagiri and Isumi. Finally, everyone was far enough away.

"Take care," Kou murmured, his voice so quiet that the two of them couldn't hear.

He gave a small quick wave.

The sight of the flower petals at the ceremony and Asagiri's smile crossed his mind briefly.

Peaceful scenes from life in the Academy revolved through his memory, but he pushed them away.

Now only Kou and the kihei remained. The membrane around its body trembled slightly, then slowly faded from cloudy white to a rusted red.

Kou steadied his breathing, knowing what was coming.

This is where things get bad.

He could tell. The kihei was expressing anger.

Kou pulled out the sword before the membrane's tremors ceased. He tumbled backward, without breaking his momentum. A slash of the membrane caressed his tracks. He tumbled to the side, slashing the grass. He didn't stop moving. As he moved, the membrane lightly brushed the back of his armor.

The impact made him stumble, but the membrane didn't reach his body.

Then, without looking back, he ran with everything he had. He had gone in the opposite direction from the others.

Kou entered farther into the ruins.

The only thing left to do was to run.

Run—until death caught up with him.

* * *

Kou continued his tragic flight. As he ran, he would sometimes fire at the walls of the ruins.

The Special Type kihei looked to be floating, but the edges of its membrane definitely touched the ground. The resulting debris was

blem was that most of the ruins repelled

armor.

"Ah, gah!"

Luckily, it didn't reach the flesh of his leg, but the impact still shattered his ankle.

Kou tumbled forward. Swallowing the agonizing pain, he scanned the surrounding area. He couldn't escape by crawling; the kihei would catch him within moments. In a split-second decision, Kou slipped out of his magic armor.

At this point, Kou Kaguro's death was almost guaranteed.

Never before had a student taken off the protective exoskeleton while on the outside and returned alive. But it bought Kou time.

"Ah!"

Now significantly slimmer, Kou twisted his body through a hole in the wall.

It looked like it had been formed recently by a natural collapse. Lucky for him, the hole was quite deep. Behind him came the sound of something slicing through the air. Kou continued forward, hoping this would pause the kihei's pursuit.

There was only darkness around him. Like a caterpillar, Kou crawled on.

That's when it happened.

He all of a sudden no longer felt anything beneath him.

Another hole had opened within the first. Unable to grab on to anything, he fell.

Something about the way he fell was strange.

It was an incredibly long fall.

Kou lost consciousness partway down before being forcibly awakened when he crashed into the reinforced glass.

Bones broke throughout his body, his organs were crushed, and he coughed up blood. Without stopping, he tumbled toward a hole broken into the glass. Unfortunately for him, his body caught on a sharp fragment jutting over the edge.

His stomach torn open, Kou fell farther into the glass structure.

Flesh and blood showered the area.

A flock of white birds took to the air all at once.

His body had come to rest in an oddly serene space.

He took his final breath.

Strangely, he wasn't afraid. He wasn't scared. He wasn't even sad.

He simply wondered whether he'd accomplished anything.

And so Kou Kaguro died.

* * *

A warm rain fell. Red droplets, slowly swallowed.

Restart in progress.

It stirred, it awoke, it operated, it knew life.

A spark in its pseudo-nervous circuit. For the first time, masses of information poured in, sweeping it away in the flood.

Joy.

Drive.

Instinct.

Longing.

Delight.

Celebration.

Nice to meet you thank you I'm sorry for the wait welcome my, my, my, my?

My gift, my nourishment, my master, my king, my servant, my joy, my fate…my Groom.

And so it opened its eyes.

The end of the world, in the form of a girl.

* * *

Kou Kaguro opened his violet eyes.

Crimson blood streamed into them.

His vision was hazy and red.

A…a persons ... g

The beautiful girl stretched out her ...

his arm in response. Intense pain shot through his entire body,

forced his hand up. Even so, she was too far.

She blinked. She ripped out the cables connected to her body and walked forward. When she reached Kou, she took his hand. Something extended from her back.

The surrounding vegetation was slashed and torn. Millions of petals fluttered about. White flowers, nearly silver, flitted through the air.

They momentarily froze before plummeting to the ground.

Amid this hallowed scene, the girl took a knee.

She pressed her lips to Kou's fingers.

"From this moment on, you are my master. My wings belong to you. I am delighted to meet you, my beloved. And oh, how I have waited for you. My name is White Princess. My alias is Curtain Call."

Just like a knight of legend, like a princess in a fairy tale, the awoken girl made an oath.

"Though you may become broken, beaten, or lost, I shall be by your side for all eternity."

Kou didn't understand what she was saying. He just felt a curiously powerful sense of familiarity.

He remembered seeing this before, in some distant dream.

Along with the shadow of a sometimes childish face and a sad face. Indeed, he remembered it.

Faint tears welled in his eyes.

Blue light fell from her wings, regenerating his wounded body. In the midst of that warmth, Kou whispered, "I feel like I've been waiting for this moment forever."

"Yes, then we are fortunate. This must be what they call fate."

The girl smiled. A look of overwhelming love spread across her inhumanly beautiful face.

It resembled the face of a mother or perhaps an elder sister.

Kou didn't know why the girl would look at him in such a way. In fact, he was confused by the words that had come out of his own mouth. But there was no time to ask anything about her.

There was a crash, and the ground shuddered. Something new had fallen into the birdcage with a great sound.

A light, veil-like membrane came into view.

Kou gaped. It was the Special Type kihei. He hadn't thought it would continue chasing him all the way here. He trembled. It wasn't just he who would be in trouble if it attacked now; the girl would be dragged into it as well.

Following Kou's gaze, the girl turned back. She saw the Special Type.

Kou frantically tried to move his broken body, but everything except his arms felt like heavy stone.

He screamed at the girl.

"Look out!" he screamed at the girl. "Run—as fast as you can!"

"What's your name?" she replied.

"Wh-what?"

"I would like to know your name."

The girl didn't respond to Kou's shouts. She looked back at him, unmoving as she waited for his answer. The kihei approached behind her. Its color flickered back to that rusted red.

It seemed the girl wouldn't move until he answered.

"It's Kou Kaguro," he shouted in a panic. "Now hurry!"

"Kou Kaguro... Registration complete. Kou, did that thing hurt you?"

She stretched out an arm, pointing at the kihei without turning back toward it.

The thing that spread from her white back swayed. Kou finally noticed the wicked-looking mechanical wings. He wondered what they were, but he didn't have time to question it. The kihei was moving in.

Which is why he simply continued to answer her questions.

"Yes, it did! That's why you need to get out of here!"

"Understood. That makes it my enemy."

The mechanical wings swished through the air.

 ̄effortlessly sliced in twain from top to

glass and was smashed

Kou stared in disbelief at what was happening in front of him.

Slowly, a gorgeous smile crept onto the girl's face.

And then she whispered:

"I give you my control, my servitude, my trust... This I swear, Kou: I will kill everything for you."

He had no idea what was going on.

Kou Kaguro temporarily lost consciousness.

they were tracing, once g
times. But she fervently wrapped her arms aro...
ture unsuited to someone trapped in such an intense malaise.

Without moving, she whispered, as if in a dream, "Once more, once more, ah… *This* time.

"*This* time, you…"

There, the voice abruptly stopped.

Followed by the sound of broken sobs.

* * *

"All right, you awake?"

Kou Kaguro opened his violet eyes.

He blinked repeatedly.

His vision was filled with white.

He realized he was in a pure-white room. There wasn't a single seam between components on the white walls, let alone a door. Kou wasn't sure how he'd even entered the room. The walls flashed blue at regular intervals. Looking closely, Kou noticed the flashing was in time with his heartbeat. That wasn't achievable with current magic technology.

This room is probably a relic from the prehistoric period, he thought.

There was very little information he could glean using his eyes alone, but he could think of no other logical conclusion.

Just then, a voice rang out from the walls themselves.

"If you're awaaaaaaake, I'd like an aaaaaaaaaaaanswer!"

The voice was absurdly loud. Kou pressed his palms over his pained ears. Whoever was speaking seemed to be able to observe him. They must be monitoring the room somehow. The next time it spoke, it was in a calm tone at a much lower volume.

"Ah, sorry. It's been a while since I've used this confinement room. It makes adjusting my voice a bit hard. Uhhh, guess this is about right? Okay... I'll remember for next time. Right. So how're your memories? Do you remember?"

"...Remember what?" asked Kou back.

The tone of the person speaking suddenly sounded far more friendly. Kou felt more on edge, wondering what was going on. Whoever was speaking remained hidden from view. But even if Kou wanted to leave the room because he didn't trust them, there were no doors.

Kou tried to sift through his memories from just before all this happened. Unexpectedly, the voice continued with something unbelievable.

"You...married a kihei, right?"

"...What?"

Kou had no clue what those words meant.

He was dumbfounded. There were a few seconds of silence. The white room flashed blue on and off in short cycles. After a moment, the speaker seemed to nod, then spoke in a voice filled with laughter.

"So you're unaware? That's not a problem. I'll explain. You came back alive from the outside, and you weren't even wearing magic armor. You came with a girl. That girl is a kihei."

"Huh?"

"And she's a real treasure. On top of that, she and you are now married."

"Married...? What in the...? Can I have a moment? There are a few points I don't understand."

"You're calm. An acceptable response, as expected from a student. Go on. Ask away once you've collected your thoughts," said the voice generously. They were going to wait until Kou had figured out the questions he wanted to ask.

The room returned to silence.

First, Kou shook his aching head. He reviewed his memories. There were no memories about coming back from the outside, but he did remember dying. Everything after that was fuzzy.

How am I even alive? he wondered.

He did, however, remember seeing something. Something stunningly beautiful.

Something white, ephemeral, and beautiful.

Kou frantically sorted his questions, then readdressed the speaker.

he wasn't a near-death hal-

more trouble for the test giver. Besides, j

tions on what's in front of you, but grasping that much in a confused state is pretty impressive, probably."

The words continued as a smooth unbroken stream, though it seemed like the man was mostly talking to himself.

Kou very much wanted to go back to his classroom. But to his surprise, the man immediately moved on to answering Kou's questions.

"Number one: The girl restarted your heart and used nanobots to completely heal your wounds. She realigned your bones while you were unconscious and reconnected them. Number two: She's a kihei. Seems that was your first time meeting a Full Humanoid kihei, but you need to just accept it for what it is. You're going to be seeing a lot of them... Then, number three."

The short explanations were followed by a foreboding statement, and Kou got the impression the man speaking had moved his hand. Or at the very least, he envisioned three fingers being held up in front of him. The casual voice continued.

"As you know, kihei kill humans. No one knows their goals or the reasons for their actions. That's just what they do. However, some of them…actually need a human master."

"…I don't understand. Those two things are contradictory. They're the enemy of humanity," said Kou.

"You're right. But it's the truth. Most humans don't have what it takes to be a kihei's master. If they run into one, they're killed immediately. But sometimes there's a human they find worthy. When that happens, they request a contract."

Kou pressed a hand to his forehead. An image of the snow-white girl appeared in his mind.

She had taken his hand and said, "From this moment on, you are my master. My wings belong to you."

"For some reason," the voice continued, *"they tend to perceive this contract as a marriage and view the other person as their spouse. We also got into the habit of calling it marriage. The kihei involved are called Brides, and the humans are called Grooms. And we call them the same thing regardless of whether the kihei is a female type or a male type—or even if they're not a humanoid type at all."*

Kou's vision swam. His brain couldn't keep up with all the new information. If it were Isumi here, he might get angry and yell at the voice to stop screwing around. But Kou understood.

For some reason, he felt like he already knew this information.

When he said to the girl, "I feel like I've been waiting for this moment forever," even then, he'd known.

Or perhaps even before then.

Ever since he had that long dream.

"So then, what I want you to decide is… Uh, what? What do you mean 'escaped'?"

The man's voice suddenly rose in pitch. Kou frowned, wondering what was happening.

At the same time, he felt like he could hear an indistinct rumbling in the distance. The man continued his conversation with another person.

"She's destroying her surroundings as she closes in on her Groom? Ah

well, that's fine. The walls on that room self-repair. That's why we went to the trouble to bring in another relic after all this time, right? And I've got a few tricks up my sleeve if it really comes down to it... Uh-oh. She's here."

There was a roaring boom.

A portion of the white in front of Kou was sliced in a circle. The round slab of thick wall fell to the ground, now practically a pillar. It was absolutely absurd. Even if the walls automatically repaired, this would take some time.

A few seconds later, Kou finally realized the wall had been sliced by someone.

He could see out through the hole. A single girl stood in a barren hallway. Her blue eyes were like the sky, her white hair like the snow. ...... of thin cloth, and she was looking at

so happy.

"Uhhh, White Princess? Could you...let me out?" he asked, ... the name he had heard when half conscious. There was no answer. He hesitantly tried knocking on the mechanical wings. The next moment, they disappeared, retreating into her back as if never there to begin with.

"You remembered my name!" she cried. She strode confidently over the rubble. The way she walked resembled that of a soldier, entirely unsuited to something that looked so ephemeral and sweet. Once in front of Kou, she brought her heels together.

A smile like a flower blooming grew on her face. It was an innocent, childlike smile.

Kou suddenly felt nostalgic. An image of someone, some childlike person, floated up from the depths of his memory, and he had the sudden sensation of a hole in his heart being filled by a perfectly sized piece.

He quietly gazed at White Princess. She stood in front of him, her palm pressed against her chest.

"I am so happy," she said. "I feel such joy when you call me by my name, as if I have become whole."

"Uhhh... That's good, right?"

"Yes, good!"

She nodded firmly, and Kou couldn't help nodding back. Their heads bobbed back and forth at each other. It created a strange, foolish display. But this was no time to be relaxing.

Kou thought back to what the man had said earlier. Very seriously, he asked, "Are you...my Bride?"

"I am! That word is exactly correct, no mistakes. You are my master. My wings belong to you. I am your Bride, and you are my Groom."

"That's..."

These sudden words left Kou flustered, but her clear eyes continued innocently looking at him. Words stuck in his throat. There was no way he could contradict her while looking at that expression.

She gently turned her blue eyes down. Solemnly, as if speaking a prayer, she whispered, "You were waiting for me, too, weren't you?"

Kou couldn't give an immediate answer. He remembered what he'd said back in the ruins: "I feel like I've been waiting for this moment forever."

Why had he said that? Even he didn't understand. Yet at the same time, he knew.

I had been waiting for someone.

For a long, long time.

There had always been a hole in his heart.

Kou opened his mouth, then closed it again.

That's when there came a hard sound from outside. Controlled footsteps approached.

"Who is that? How rude," said White Princess as she gracefully turned back.

"...What's happening now?" asked Kou, turning his gaze.

A strange group entered through the hole in the wall.

Their characteristic vermilion-and-black uniforms resembled those of the military, and long cloaks swayed from their backs.

Their faces were hidden behind masks. Foxes, cats, crows, and the like, their eyes painted in vermilion. None of them looked like full-grown adults. They looked strange, but they were likely students, like Kou.

Kou narrowed his eyes. He put himself between White Princess and the group. He knew she was strong, but he couldn't abandon her. White Princess hopped, perhaps because Kou was blocking her view.

"Kou, are these people your enemies?" she asked sullenly.

"I don't know yet."

"Then I will set their enemy status as uncertain. I can implement their destruction immediately anyway."

Kou shuddered. He didn't get the sense that she was lying. She had ... before them. He clenched

anyway. And also, this is really imp...

Kou's words cut off there for a moment. He pushed throught the complicated emotions that were suddenly bursting forth inside him.

Once he found his answer, he stared deep into her blue eyes. Sincere and straightforward, he told her, "I don't want to see you kill people."

"What?"

Her eyes grew round. She looked extremely confused. But that was truly how Kou felt. Not much time had passed since they met, but he knew that he couldn't bear the thought of her white becoming stained with red.

He wasn't certain why, but everything inside him rejected that possibility.

"Please, White Princess. I…don't want you to do that kind of thing."

"Understood. I give you my control, my servitude, my trust… There is value in listening to your words."

She nodded, and the hostility that roiled from her entire being faded.

Kou felt the stress drop from his body like a ton of bricks.

It seemed her antagonism had put him subconsciously on edge. The students surrounding them, however, had not let down their guard. Swords, guns, and other weapons remained at the ready.

Tension filled the room. Then came some half-hearted applause, followed by a casual voice.

"That's enough. You pass, you pass. Well, I think we already knew you would. We already received the report of you saving the Research squad by acting as bait. A good person is valuable. As of right now, you're not humanity's enemy, or the end of the world, and you can't be... So then."

It was the voice that had come from the walls earlier.

Another intruder appeared in the room.

Kou gulped. He was a slender man with white hair, one blue eye, and one black. That color combination must be fairly rare in nature. His bangs were long, and the rest of his hair was cut roughly. Deep scars stood prominently on his face and neck. His heavily decorated military uniform was covered with a worn, shabby coat. He looked suspicious.

Kou narrowed his eyes in distrust, and that wasn't only from the man's questionable appearance.

Kou was struck by a strange impression.

He could swear he'd seen that man's face somewhere.

At the same time, that face didn't match any he'd ever seen.

The man swayed as he walked, the hem of his coat moving this way and that, before stopping in front of Kou.

"I want you to choose," he said. "I can kill you. Which makes that the first option. Dying here."

He smiled; White Princess was reflected in his eyes. Kou found the man's expression astonishing; he was genuinely telling the truth. He likely could kill not only Kou but also White Princess.

Kou spread his arms in front of her, though he knew it was pointless.

She hopped behind him again.

The man's eyes narrowed, and he nodded. For some reason, he sounded incredibly bored as he continued.

*   *   *

"Or you can come with us and watch hell burn for what feels like an eternity."

Kou couldn't tell which choice was more horrible.
The man calmly presented the options to Kou.
His empty eyes pierced the two of them.
Like he was looking at the carcass of a dead insect, Kou thought.

* * *

"You know, I don't get this whole 'I don't want to die' mentality," said the man suddenly as he led the way in front of them.

He waved the fingers of one hand meaninglessly and continued his monologue. "It's true, death is one of humanity's ultimate riddles. Nobody knows what happens once the function of life halts. That's why people invent gods and cling to the life after. But even so, they still don't want to die. All this despite the fact that we don't have the means to prove that living is easier. Don't you agree? By the way, this is all just a bunch of nonsense, so you don't actually have to listen to me. Though, I'd be happy if you did."

"…Uh-huh."

Kou gave a noncommittal response. The man pouted in disappointment. It wasn't a particularly cute expression when made by a full-grown man. It might even be moving into creepy territory.

Kou wasn't certain how he should respond.

He chose silence. He looked around them. They hadn't passed any people in a while. A luxurious carpet covered the hallway's floor, and the walls and window frames were decorated with carvings. The building's interior was imposing and old-fashioned. Or so it looked at first. In fact, all this was the work of 3D images created by cutting-edge magic crystals.

Based on how fancy the equipment is, Kou thought, *I can only assume this is Central Headquarters.*

Behind him followed the attackers from earlier, still in their masks and remaining silent. Kou and White Princess walked with this group like prisoners being escorted down the hallway. Everything about the situation he'd found himself in was unpleasant and incomprehensible.

And there was one other thing he didn't understand.

"Huh?"

"Hmm?"

For a while now, White Princess had been walking while practically hanging from his arm, her soft chest pressed against him. A vaguely pleasant scent wafted from her silvery-white hair.

As he tried to keep his composure, he asked, "Why are you walking so close to me?"

"When that man becomes aggressive toward you, I will act as your

reme than he'd expected.

analysis

continued to evaluate options wit

cessfully saving your life should *that* become aggressive. My

unavoidable, no matter which option I choose."

Her expression was tense. While her words were alarming, there was something about her expression that was innocent.

But it was obvious that she felt strong determination as she said, "In which case, I can only choose. This is a serious situation, and not light—"

"Stop, please. If you die, it doesn't matter if you protect me or not; I won't be happy!" shouted Kou.

"Understood. If you don't like it, it's bad."

Unexpectedly, she immediately backed down. Kou let out a sigh of relief.

Just thinking of the possibility made Kou feel like there was a burning coal in the pit of his stomach. He clenched his fists. If that happened, he would never be able to forgive himself. Yes, he felt deep unease imagining her sacrifice.

Though he didn't know why.

But he was sure he couldn't bear it.

There came a laid-back voice from ahead of them. Looking in that direction, Kou saw the man jumping up and down.

"Listen already, I'm not going to kill you! What do you take me for? Some maniac who murders his own students?"

"Would you please just shut up—? Uh…students?" said Kou.

"Oh, now you're getting bossy with me? What a drag," said the man.

A question had appeared in Kou's mind. In front of him, the man fiddled with the hem of his coat. It was definitely a creepy mannerism. He stopped moving for a moment when Kou asked his question and nodded.

"Yep. My students. That reminds me, I haven't even told you my name. I'm Kagura."

Just Kagura.

Kou gasped when he heard the name. He'd heard it before. Kagura was the most powerful and most admired teacher in the Academy. Being placed under Kagura could only mean being assigned to the Elite Squad immediately under his command.

Kou wondered how that could be. At the same time, he looked back at White Princess. It must have something to do with her presence. She was powerful enough to defeat a Special Type kihei single-handedly.

That sort of strength went far beyond what even the Combat students could handle.

Before Kou could say anything, Kagura continued.

"Yep, very perceptive. Being my students means you're in my squad. It's not just an elite unit, though. Just being excellent in battle isn't enough to get you in." Kagura's words cut off there. His lips curled into a smile. He meaninglessly waved his fingers through the air, then in a booming voice said, "This is the 'nonexistent' class one hundred of the Department of Combat, a special squad made only from people married to kihei."

He abruptly started walking again, and suddenly they were at the

end of the hallway, in front of a single door. He gripped the doorknob
and pulled open the door.

"…Welcome to Pandemonium."

Kou's eyes opened wide. The classroom was constructed the same as
the largest standard lecture hall he'd seen, but there were no windows.
Behind the circular rows of chairs were huge piles of what looked like
the students' personal belongings.

And there were things scattered about that just weren't supposed to
be there.

⸺ be seen in the room.

⸺ 's chairs was like some sort of

⸺ Kihei waiting

Curiosity, ⸺

Eyes filled with all differe⸺

White Princess.

* * *

A moment later, there was a surge of lively voices behind Kou and
White Princess. The group of mask wearers was talking. They relaxed
their wariness the moment they stepped through the door, like they'd
been dismissed from duty.

They walked off wherever they liked as they chattered.

"Oh man, I'm exhausted. Absolutely beat!"

"Escorting a Groom with a Princess Series is no joke. He needs to
just do it himself, then die."

"I was so nervous. But Mr. Most Powerful didn't want to go alone!
What a whiny baby."

"My shoulders are so stiff. Seriously. Teacher, give me a massage."

"No! Get your wife to do it!"

"She'd turn my shoulders into mincemeat."

One after another, the students removed their masks. The faces beneath were those of typical boys and girls. The statuesque squad from before quickly turned into something more human. Kou blinked in surprise.

Below the masks were people who looked far more like average students than he'd expected. Each one of them was apparently a member of Pandemonium. They moved into the classroom and selected a seat to sit in.

As each of them settled into a spot, they clapped their hands once, snapped their fingers, or clicked their heels.

"All right, come out, my lady."

"Good job and thank you, my dear."

Brides appeared around the students as the kihei were called forth one after another. They all looked different. There was one that resembled a snake, one that looked like a scorpion, even humanoid ones. All categories were represented: Type A, Type B, and Special Type.

Kou took a step back, struck by an instinctual fear that sent a shiver down his spine. If they felt like it, the kihei here were enough to kill every single student in the Department of Magic Research. That's how many kihei there were in the room—and how powerful they were.

Kou felt dizzy. Kagura placed a hand on the shoulder of one of the students in front of Kou and explained, despite the student's obvious resistance.

"These kids are the ones married to Brides that can conceal themselves. It can be kind of a pain to run into other people in headquarters with a kihei in tow. That's why I asked them to help me escort you... Ah, oh, you're going? But now I'm lonely!"

The red-haired student escaped from Kagura, who flapped the hem of his coat. The other students shot complaints back at the teacher, telling him to stop that—that it wasn't cute. Turned out his mannerisms weren't popular within Pandemonium, either.

While the students and Kagura had their casual exchange, Kou still felt beads of cold sweat run down his spine.

I didn't even realize there were kihei there, he thought.

The Department of Combat's database did include information on kihei that could conceal themselves, but the vast majority of students never encountered one. If they were on the outside right now, Kou would already be dead.

But then Kou began to rethink that. So long as White Princess was there, things might go differently. Because she would protect him. This girl, who was apparently a kihei, was still full of mysteries, but he was starting to view her as precious to him. He felt close to her in a way that surprised even himself. But it still hadn't hit him yet that she was his Bride.

He looked at her.

She smiled broadly at him, though he didn't know what she was thinking. Uncertain what to do, he gave a weak smile back. Her smile deepened, like a flower blooming. It was lovely expression.

Watching them, someone snorted from their seat and said, "It's get-

could easily see it happening.

Again, Kou hid White Princess behind his back, moving on impulse. He had to protect her; nothing else mattered.

Paying this no heed, Kagura gave Kou a cheery pat on the back, then pointed at White Princess and said, "So here are our new transfer students! This is Kou Kaguro, and this is White Princess. As you all know, she's a Princess Series, the most powerful type of kihei, and she's the previously unconfirmed seventh member of the series. Her alias is—"

"Curtain Call," said White Princess.

"There you have it! With your excellent perception, I bet you have a bad feeling about what's next. Ah-ha-ha-ha!"

Kou didn't understand what Kagura was saying, especially his cheerful laugh.

He decided Kagura was off his rocker. What did those words even mean? Animosity grew stronger in the eyes of the members of Pandemonium, causing Kou to recoil slightly. The air was thick with tension.

Silver ~~~~
hair cascaded over her skin. Every time ~~~
hair spilled to the ground.

Numerous clocks decorated her surroundings. Clocks that used sand, clocks that matched the movement of the stars, clocks that expressed the time of the spirits, even clocks from prehistory with different motions. But they all had one thing in common.

All the clocks were moving too slow.

But she was used to that.

Time was not her ally; she knew that well.

She would continue to wait alone until the clocks rang again.

She slowly closed her black eyes.

It was cold.

It was dark.

And it was lonely.

* * *

There was a sharp *shing* of metal.

The blade scraped, releasing a shower of golden sparks.

Kou was wielding a strange sword. The grip was slender, but the sword spread out wider as it extended. The full thing resembled the shape of a bird's feather, as it should.

This was a feather taken from White Princess's wings. He was using it as a weapon. It was filled with magic—magic that wasn't Kou's.

Each time he swung the sword, traces of flames rushed out into the air.

It was a powerful weapon, but Kou wasn't in a good position, even with it in hand.

He shifted his sword and wiped away the sweat running down his brow.

White Princess hung back behind Kou, her mechanical wings unfurled.

She looked somewhat different from before. Instead of the thin cloth that used to wrap her body, she now wore a white suit fashioned like a military uniform. The cuffs and chest were decorated with what some might call overly ornate fabric and ribbons.

It suited one called a Bride. It also made Kou think of the holy shrine maidens in the imperial capital.

White Princess wasn't currently fighting. Instead, she was acting only as Kou's support.

And there, in front of the two of them, was a monster.

It was a gigantic kihei. Its bones were metal, its flesh made from a mixture of organic material and stone. It was likely a Type A kihei, though leaning toward a Special Type. It resembled a golem, beings made of stone and possessed by spirits, but only in appearance.

The giant's head was dangerously close to the classroom's ceiling. Every once in a while, the stone edge scraped against it, producing a sound.

In front of "him" was a small young girl.

Just like White Princess, the girl wore a modified military uniform. Her skirt had layers of complicated frills, and there was a flower decoration at her throat. She had voluminous, soft blond hair and jade-colored eyes that looked like a fairy's.

Her sweet voice matched her appearance, but the words she spoke didn't.

"Seems you can handle yourself. I'm trying to crush you, but I can't. Boring, uninteresting, uncute, unpleasant. I don't understand. Why won't you just die?"

Her face was nearly expressionless. She really just wondered why.

Following her hostile question came a shout from somewhere in the room. It was a boy, and he issued a warning.

"Tsubaki, no killing. Kagura will murder you if you do. Or are you fine with that?"

"Be quiet, Hikami," said the girl. "Besides, I can't crush him even if I try. Which means that it doesn't matter how much I think about crushing him. That's freedom of thought."

...ing around. I really can't handle this," replied

For some time ...

place, only Kou was being run down.

She eyed him coldly. Her cute lips curled into a sarcastic sneer.

"Shut up," she said. "You're Phantom Rank; that's higher than my Demon Rank. If you really have what it takes, then of course you can handle this much. Getting injured would prove you're not qualified, and dying would mean you're in way over your head. That's all I'm saying. Now just come to terms with this: I'm going to do my best to crush you, but you won't be crushed. And then fight back with everything you have. I'll crush you."

"Kou, this girl is a potential enemy. Shall I kill her?" asked White Princess.

"Absolutely not. Besides, this fight is between her and me; the kihei are being kept back. That's how this is done," said Kou.

White Princess puffed up her cheeks, while Tsubaki bobbed her head in agreement.

This battle was between only the Grooms, though they were borrowing their kihei's power. That was the rule. And in fact, Tsubaki hadn't ordered her Bride to act.

With a dramatic gesture, she snapped her fingers.

"If you're not going to come at me, then I'll make the first move. I'll crush you."

As she did that, a stone wall appeared in front of Kou. It tilted over in an attempt to crush him.

Kou quickly thrust his blade into the joint where two stones met. The stones were bonded together with a fleshy gelatin, to which he set fire. Some of it melted, and the wall collapsed. Having somehow withstood this attack, he let out a ragged breath.

For some reason, Tsubaki nodded in satisfaction, her beautiful blond hair bouncing.

Jeers and cheers rang out from all directions at once as people voiced their personal opinions one after the other.

"Not bad, not bad. I'm betting on the newbie."

"I'll put one down for Tsubaki."

"This doesn't happen every day. Fight back like you want to kill!"

"I'm waiting for a one-hit finish."

"I think we might have an upset."

Kagura, on the other hand, stood in place with his arms crossed. His posture was one of quiet observation.

Kou's thoughts spun. Why the hell was he doing this? How did he get here?

* * *

The Princess Series, the most powerful of all kihei.

The seventh member of the series, whose existence was previously unconfirmed.

Alias: Curtain Call.

After some words that Kou didn't understand, the atmosphere in the classroom became even less welcoming. But it was headed toward an even more decisive change.

Kagura continued with another declaration.

"All right, about Kou Kaguro's rank—he's going to be Phantom. That makes him the fourth one."

The classroom burst into noisy chatter. Kou looked around, wondering what was going on.

All twenty-five of the students were letting themselves be heard, without banding together. Blatant dissatisfaction showed on all their faces. They seemed to have strong feelings about this. One of them raised their hand.

He was a red-haired boy with an eye patch over one eye. His uniform was largely unmodified.

In a deep voice that matched the levelheaded impression he gave, he said, "Can I ask a question?"

"Yes, Hikami, ask away. I think I know what you're going to ask, but

five of you, and with another

The student named Hikami narrowed his already sharp eye.

The ruckus in the classroom grew even louder.

Kagura's words made Kou shudder. Kou had heard that Pandemonium, the Elite Squad commanded by Kagura, was the most powerful in the school. He didn't think he could kill even one of them.

More importantly, he had no hostile intentions.

"Hold on. I don't plan on killing anyone," said Kou.

"I know."

"Coward."

"Get out of here."

"That fight lacked spirit. I call for a do-over."

Impressive insults came flying at Kou. He pressed a hand to his aching forehead. White Princess fidgeted and asked if this was a show of hostility. While holding her back, Kou mustered the least irritated voice he could and told the students, "If I even thought about killing you, you'd all come at me at once, right? So there's no reason for all these insults and criticisms."

"I know."

"Correct."

"Good point."

"That's the spirit I'm looking for."

The reaction was surprisingly positive. Kou let out a frustrated sigh, completely unable to understand.

That's when one of the female students smoothly raised her hand.

"…Excuse me. May I speak?"

She stood, a slim young woman with distinctive, gentle eyes. Her glossy chestnut-colored hair fell softly over her shoulders. She was tall with a narrow waist. The skirt hemline of her uniform was more like a full-length dress.

There was something about her appearance that felt graceful and elegant. She brought a hand to her ample bosom and spoke mildly.

"Professor, it appears that Kou Kaguro is confused. I believe he first requires an explanation of the rank system. Since you're so unreliable, I would like to offer the explanation myself."

"Thank you for the apt comment and the insult, Mirei," said Kagura. "…Huh? Thank you? That makes me sound like a masochist… Uh, well anyway. It's fine! Explain away!"

"It's all right; I'll turn you into a real masochist someday. Now, Kou Kaguro. Pleased to meet you. My name is Mirei Tachibana. Have no fear and surrender yourself to my explanation."

"Scary," muttered Kou without thinking. Mirei smiled slightly, despite likely having heard. Her expression held no hostility. She snapped her fingers, and a kihei that had been lying down below her seat sat up.

Kou couldn't help gulping. It was a Special Type Bride.

Its entire body was bound in chains. Every inch of the vaguely humanoid figure was cruelly restrained.

Mirei pulled on her Bride's chains and exuberantly said, "First, let me introduce you. This is my Bride. His alias is My Kitty. He's pleased to make your acquaintance. The chains really suit him, don't you think? So cute! Go ahead and compliment him, I don't mind. Hee-hee-hee."

Mirei squeezed her Bride in a hug.

It was wrapped in chains with an iron ball stuffed in what looked to be its mouth, but it let out a meow like a cat. Mirei rubbed her cheek against "him." The deep love between them was obvious from their affectionate display, but Mirei suddenly drew her hand away. My Kitty disappeared below the chair with a thud.

Mirei then stepped on her Bride, in a gesture filled to the brim with love.

Kou couldn't stop the rain of cold sweat running down his spine. Mirei continued as if nothing had happened.

"Now I'll start an explanation of the rank system."

"What should I do? I don't think the information's going to stick in my brain…," said Kou.

"Try your best. Each of us is given a rank matching our strength. The

selves. Three or more of them can handle a Type A, and it is recommended that either six or more handle a Special Type, or they flee. A Wasp Rank can handle either a Type A or a Type B on their own, while three Wasp Ranks can handle a Special Type. A Demon Rank can handle all types of kihei on their own. And a Phantom Rank…'must surpass all.'"

Mirei delivered her explanation sedately. The content made Kou's face pale.

A regular student could handle a Type B kihei so long as they were wearing magic armor. But as for Type A or Special types, even if multiple students worked together, they would all wind up dead.

If the Department of Combat gathered a dozen or so of its experienced students, they could probably manage to destroy a Special Type, but it would inevitably end with a lot of casualties. It was also likely that things would go poorly, and they would all die.

It was outside the realm of what was humanly possible for someone to handle one of those alone—and without armor as well. When it came to Phantom Rank, Kou was completely unable to so much as imagine that amount of power. Yet unbelievably, he was somehow already one of them.

Touching a hand to her chest, Mirei continued smoothly.

"I, Mirei Tachibana, am Demon Rank. Hikami, the boy from a moment ago, is Wasp Rank. The others...well, you can try to ask for yourself if you have the opportunity."

Mirei surveyed the classroom and smiled. She likely decided the others wouldn't reply even if she called on them. A few of them struck meaningless poses of celebration.

Kou wondered how long it would take to get to know all of them and let out a small internal sigh.

Mirei's smile suddenly disappeared. Her eyes, the same color as her hair, gleamed as she asked, "We have had transfer students before, but most of them have been Flower Rank; the highest only reached Wasp Rank. I have a hard time accepting that you could jump immediately to Phantom Rank. What has led to this assignment, I wonder?"

"The truth is obvious. I am the most powerful Bride here," White Princess boasted. The classroom broke into an uproar again. Kou quickly spun back to her, but she looked completely unfazed, with no signs of excitement. She was just stating the facts as they were.

Mirei nodded gently, though her voice was threatening as she continued.

"Yes, that may be so. Even a Special Type is like garbage to a Princess Series; they're on a different level. And when it comes to you...the seventh in the series, we aren't even certain of your true abilities."

Kou's eyes widened. Kagura had just said something about the Princess Series being the most powerful of the kihei. Kou looked at White Princess, wondering if that was really true.

She smiled, as if to say it was obvious.

Mirei looked around the classroom, briefly shook her head, and whispered, "It's true that the only one who could hope to defeat you would be our other Phantom Rank who took a Princess as their Bride. They're not here at the moment, incidentally. But these ranks also take into consideration the ability of the Groom… With that in mind, I think a rank of Demon would be appropriate."

"But Kou is stronger than the majority of the people here," said White Princess.

"Huh?"

The one most taken aback by this statement was Kou himself, but White Princess's expression remained unchanged. It appeared she wasn't just trying to show off. She nodded as she spoke, pride in her voice.

"I have completed my analysis. His abilities are comparable to a Demon Rank Groom. Bearing that in mind, and including my strength as well, this Phantom Rank, as you call it, would be the most suitable. I see nothing wrong with Kagura's conclusion," she said.

At first glance, she looked like a doll. Her small body was sitting on the shoulder of a giant, her arm tangled in her blond hair as she rested her chin on her fist. She glared down like a queen from her throne at not only Kou but also Kagura.

Her jade-colored eyes blinked like those of a capricious kitten.

In response, Kagura flatly said, "Yes, go ahead, Tsubaki."

"We're having an exam, right? If he's Phantom Rank, then I can do it. That should be appropriate," she said, though Kou didn't understand the implications of her words.

Her commanding tone didn't suit her innocent appearance. Her jade eyes narrowed. She stared at Kou, as if she were sizing him up.

There seemed to be a hint of sadness in her voice as she spoke.

"This talk of Phantom Rank is interesting. If he's worthy, then that's fine. But if he's unsuited to his Bride, then he can't do his job when it comes to protecting and being protected. That would be bad for both of them. If that's the case, then we can't accept his transfer. If it's his fate to be crushed at some point, then let me be the one to put an end to it. That'd be the merciful thing to do."

Her severe tone belied her cute appearance. Her jade eyes closed gently, then opened. She stood up on the giant's shoulder. Her frilly skirt gently swelled. She pointed at Kou with a swish of her blond hair.

Her grand declaration of war echoed through the classroom.

"I, Demon Rank Tsubaki Kagerou, will crush him."

The room burst with activity, voices boiling up from all over the classroom. Oddly, they contained no ill will. Instead, Kou glimpsed a kind of unrestrained cheer, like children enjoying a festival.

The students closer to the lectern stood and quickly began rearranging the room. It seemed the majority of them were excited by this turn of events.

Kou looked around, his eyes seeking an explanation of what was happening. Kagura responded with a detached tone.

"Well, there's this kind of tradition sort of thing where transfers fight against another student, either in the same rank or lower. Can't really let students transfer to Pandemonium if they don't fit in. Think of it like a rite of passage and just resign yourself to it. Tsubaki's going to be your opponent today."

"… Isn't this a little rushed? I didn't even agree."

Kou swept his eyes over the classroom. The only person who seemed distressed over the situation was Mirei, who stood with a hand on her cheek. He shot her an imploring look. He didn't like fighting; he needed to find someone who could stop this.

After mulling over something for a while, Mirei said, "I don't mind if you fight, but I do think White Princess needs a wardrobe change first."

"O-oh," replied Kou, hanging his head in disappointment.

"Mm, that is acceptable," said White Princess with a nod.

She closed her eyes and caused the cloth that wrapped around her to change. First, it became a matching Pandemonium uniform, then the color faded to white, and decorations were added per White Princess's wishes. Blue light surrounded her and burst out.

White Princess remained standing, body now wrapped in an adorable outfit.

Kou stared at her new clothing and couldn't stop himself from asking, "Do you like those kinds of clothes?"

"Yes, they suit me the best. But more importantly, it seems you'll have to fight, Kou."

"As much as I don't want to, yeah," he said bitterly.

He knew that if he refused, there would be no more welcomes. There was no way he could avoid this fight if he was going to join Pandemonium.

The giant walked slowly down the stairs, still carrying Tsubaki. They stopped in front of the lectern among the half-joking cheers of the students.

Kou got an explanation of the rules next, then...

Just like that, we ended up here.

* * *

"Come on, now, is that all? That's not even enough to rival a Demon Rank!"

Tsubaki was chattering in her high-pitched voice. She waved her finger in a little dance.

Walls flew at Kou again, this time from the left and right. He ducked his head to evade them so they slammed into one another. Then he flipped out from underneath and kicked the new wall that had appeared in the air above. And using the counterforce from his kick, he pierced the wall behind him with his sword.

Each time he made a move, jeers and cheers bubbled up in the classroom.

"Go get 'em!"

"Not too bad!"

"Still slow."

"Nothing unexpected."

"He needs a little more speed."

Somehow, Kou managed to keep slicing the walls apart. But as someone so accurately pointed out, he didn't have much leeway in his motions. Tsubaki's ridicule was only natural. What she'd said about an unsuitable match being bad for both Bride and Groom was absolutely correct.

Kou Kaguro didn't have the fighting skills necessary for handling attacks like this. Which is why he'd been starting to feel…incredibly at peace with the situation.

I'm starting to get it… My field of vision is too narrow, he thought, realizing one of the reasons he was at a disadvantage.

Humans had just two eyes. Obviously, that meant there was a limit to what they could take in.

all of Tsubaki's walls coming from every possible experienced to grasp their location do about that, or

A separat

It was a view from behind

himself and Tsubaki. And his sword moved

mation, faster than he could have reacted himself.

By subconsciously using these two things, he had been handling walls that appeared in locations he couldn't see.

Kou had an idea where this viewpoint was coming from.

…This is White Princess's "sight."

The two had become connected before he even knew it. Bride and Groom, joined together.

And if that's the case!

He fully shifted his vision to take in hers instead and continued to use her sight. Then he relaxed his body and let the sword guide his movements.

"…Not bad."

"Yep."

"Huh, that's unexpected."

"Ah, their synchrony is abnormally high. That's not the kind of cooperation you'd expect from someone who's just met their Bride."

Kou could hear voices coming from somewhere, but he didn't have the extra focus needed to determine who said what. The walls were appearing more quickly and moving faster now. The sword was demanding quicker reactions.

Just a single moment of diverted attention could seal his fate.

"—!"

He kicked off a wall coming from above and rotated. With legs spread and body flat, he cut apart a wall below him. Pulling the sword back up, he rolled to the right and pierced the wall on the left. His mind was blank as he moved.

He went as fast as he could go, slicing through wall after wall.

As Tsubaki watched him, her previously expressionless face began to change. A strange joy creeped into her jade eyes. She hadn't been seriously fighting until now. She had said she would crush Kou, but her moves up to now could hardly be called aggressive.

Things were changing now.

A wicked smile spread across Tsubaki's face. "Ah, good!" she squealed. "It's not cute, it's not lovely, but it's not bad either! Now let's get serious! I, Tsubaki Kagerou, will crush you, here and now!"

Walls immediately appeared around Kou in every direction, forming a caved-in sphere with Kou at the center.

I can't dodge this!

Neither did he have time to destroy a section. The next moment, the walls closed in on each other.

With Kou in the middle.

The floating stone sphere was complete.

The boy named Hikami shouted, "That's enough! He might be dead! I'm going to help him; you mind?"

Kou heard the voice from where he was inside the sphere.

Using his sword as a prop, he had managed to keep the sphere from closing completely. He considered the situation. Tsubaki was probably distracted by Hikami's shouting. Either that or she had assumed she finished Kou off and let her guard down.

Kou knew his chance was now or never.

He whispered, "White Princess... Give me another feather."

"Understood, Kou. I give you my control, my support. Everything I am is yours."

Even from inside the stone, Kou knew that White Princess had immediately released a feather from her wing. It pierced into the sphere from the outside. Kou pushed his own sword into the wall from the inside. It was a tandem attack from both sides.

The magic within the feathers was fire and ice, and the violent reaction between the two exploded the sphere. The walls shattered into fragments and flew in every direction.

Kou planted his feet on a shard of rubble just before it began to fall. _____ his legs and leaped with explosive force, zipping through the

The feather had been stopped by Kagura.

Kou blinked. He didn't understand what had happened. It was hard to believe that Kagura could have stopped the blade with his bare hand. With the way things were going, he should have stabbed Tsubaki. Looking carefully, though, Kou caught sight of a magic circle on Kagura's palm. It was completely blocking White Princess's feather.

Kou eventually calmed. Then a shudder hit him.

It's a good thing Kagura stopped the sword... I lost control of myself.

He had told White Princess that he didn't want to see people die, and now he was about to kill someone himself?

He repeated one phrase in his mind as he wiped the cold sweat from his brow.

The fight is over.

He had somehow managed to end it. That much he understood.

His feet came to the ground with a thud.

The classroom exploded into cheers.

* * *

"Sorry I jumped in back there… But that was more than enough. There should be no problem declaring the transfer student the winner, with that performance and no experience. And no one got hurt, either. Not bad," said Hikami.

"I agree; I accept that you're comparable to a Demon Rank. That was fun, wasn't it?" added Mirei.

The other students were just as welcoming, for the most part.

Kou steadied his breathing. His senses were quickly coming back to him.

As they did, they brought a question.

He still didn't fully understand what had happened. That was his first time experiencing a fight alongside a kihei, and he had totally lost himself in it. He didn't even comprehend his own actions.

He thought back to what happened in the fight. It had felt like the movements of someone else, not his own.

…Like I knew how to fight from the start.

He was perplexed by how that could be.

As he thought, he was suddenly enveloped by something. Mechanical objects obscured his vision, though they were objects he recognized. Those were White Princess's wings. He knocked on the surface.

While still in his daze, he said, "White Princess, White Princess, can you let me out?"

"Aaah, I expected no less from my Kou! I knew that my wings were one with you… Though, to be honest, I was afraid for a moment. If by some chance you died, I would self-destruct on the spot."

"No self-destructing. Absolutely not," said Kou.

"No?"

"No. I don't like it, so you can't do it… Come on, now, White Princess, calm down," he said gently as he tapped on her wings again.

Eventually, very hesitantly, she opened her mechanical wings, then stood stock-still, staring up at him. There were tears gathered in the rims of her beautiful blue eyes. It was so strange. White Princess was so powerful she didn't need to fear anything, yet it seemed like she couldn't help worrying about him.

Kou drew her into a hug, as if it were the natural thing to do. He patted her back as he tried to calm her.

"...Kou?" she asked.

"Don't worry; everything's okay now." Affection welled inside him. In his gratitude, he said, "Thank you, White Princess... I won, somehow. It's all thanks to you."

The words came from the bottom of his heart. If she hadn't been there, he wouldn't have managed to handle even a single attack.

Victory was within reach because she fought with him. He tightly embraced her, the girl who walked the line of death with him. She returned his hug. Even so, Kou was still unsure.

"... ... ...?" he asked.

didn't change the fact that ... g

Kou then turned to look at Tsubaki. She was smiling, even though she'd lost. For some reason, she looked satisfied. The annoyed expression she'd had when she challenged Kou was gone.

Whether he liked it or not, he understood.

The people in Pandemonium were just like this.

Kagura clapped his hands together loudly, then said, "All right. With that... We are the proud members of Pandemonium. We lie in the dark, spoken ill of by others. Our Brides and our skills are everything... And I assume there are no objections to him joining us."

"None from me."

"Nope."

"He's not bad."

"If I had to pick, I'd say I approve."

There were multiple replies.

Some of them crossed their legs, some grinned, some remained hunched over their desk...but all expressed agreement.

Kou wiped away his sweat that wouldn't stop and nodded.

On the edge of this eternal hell or whatever it was, it seemed like they'd finally secured their place.

Over these long, long years, still pursued it.

Even though she knew it would fall apart, like reaching out toward a tower built on sand.

* * *

"All right, this is the assigned room for you two! Go on in!" said Kagura in high spirits as he opened the door, revealing an opulent room.

They were in a corner of Central Headquarters' left wing.

The fight with Tsubaki had ended just as it was time for Pandemonium's classes to wrap up for the day. They were then allowed free time.

Kagura decided Kou must be tired, since it was his first day, and showed him to his dorm room.

When they reached the correct door, Kou stopped and stared in amazement.

The floor was covered in a plush carpet, the bed decorated with a canopy. All the other furniture was just as old-fashioned looking. They seemed to be real antiques. The room must have been decorated without regard to cost, focusing entirely on comfort.

The decorations were, from another perspective, utterly ridiculous.

Kou pointed into the room and timidly asked, "This…isn't actually a 'dorm' room, is it?"

"Ah, you noticed? It's because our class *doesn't exist*. There aren't actually any dorms in Central Headquarters. So we've taken the number of guest rooms we need and designated them as dorm rooms. There's also a Pandemonium-exclusive kitchen and dining hall! Let me know if there's anything you find inconvenient. Your teacher's super accommodating!"

With a wave, Kagura turned to go, but Kou clamped his hand onto Kagura's shoulder. The teacher remained silent and continued trying to make his exit, but Kou physically dragged him back over to the room.

Facing Kagura head-on, Kou said, "There's only one bed."

"Correct," said Kagura.

"Are you telling me to sleep with White Princess?"

"Well, you two are husband and wife. Isn't that how it should be?"

"I find that statement lacking in moral character."

Kou instinctively disapproved. The custom of a girl and boy who'd only recently met sharing a bed was completely foreign to him.

But Kagura, a teacher no less, just laughed it off like it was fine. Kou opened his mouth to complain again, but Kagura's attitude changed immediately. His words were cold.

"I told you, didn't I? She looks like a human, but she's not. She's a kihei."

"Well…yeah."

"To tell you the truth, this is also the second exam. Controlling each Bride comes down to the Groom. You've been given a duty, 'in sickness and in health.' There are no exceptions. And that means we need proof that you won't let your Bride run rampant through Central Headquarters."

Kou swallowed. What Kagura said was true.

A kihei couldn't be allowed out in Central Headquarters unsupervised. Kou understood that rule. Even so, Kou tried to continue his protest. This time, Kagura grinned.

"Hey, I get how you feel. White Princess is super cute, yeah?"

"Yes, I am cute. Because I am Kou's Bride. I'm sure I am of an appropriate cuteness," said White Princess.

"That's not... I mean, yes, she is cute, but don't make fun of the issue here!" said Kou urgently.

Kagura flapped the hem of his shabby coat. He pouted like he thought this was a lot of trouble over nothing, then interrupted and ___ the conversation over. Fluttering his hand in a wave, he said, ___ I'm just telling the truth! Anyway, I obviously ___ For starters, just focus on getting ___ for your intellec-

and ___

She squeezed her ___

said, "I won't mind, no matter wh___

"Okay, White Princess! Don't say that when yo___ what's going on!"

He placed his hands on her shoulders as he spoke. Incredibly exhausted, he looked around the room.

Luckily, there was a sofa perfectly suited for lying on. He secretly decided that he would sleep there. There was a fully stocked bathroom next to the sofa. He reentered the room with White Princess and closed the door.

Think I'll take a shower and hit the hay, thought Kou.

He looked back to find White Princess jumping on the bed. The next moment, she was rolling around back and forth on it. It seemed like her first encounter with furniture was going very well.

Lying on her back, she said, "Kou, this is so comfortable. It's soft and nice."

"That's good, White Princess. You can have the bed—"

"What are you saying?" She cocked her head and innocently picked up a pillow. She squeezed it to herself like it was precious and gently continued, "If you're ready, then let's sleep together. I'm sure it'll be fun."

She gave a smile that could rival the most beautiful flowers.

For Kou, however, that was a bombshell statement.

* * *

"No."

"Why?"

"I refuse."

"But why?"

"Please at least consider a boy's feelings."

"The heart is difficult to understand. I also don't understand why you are trying to sleep apart from me."

After Kou had taken a shower and caught his breath, the real battle between White Princess and him had begun.

And of all things, she had changed back into the thin fabric from before. It seemed she had chosen it while searching for 'clothes to relax in.' For a while now, she'd been patting the bed beside her with her hands as if to say there was plenty of space for them both. But Kou dug in his heels.

"Kou, it's fine, isn't it?"

"No, it is not."

White Princess puffed up her cheeks. Her long hair swished as she hopped.

She tried to wrap her arms around him. He hurriedly sidestepped.

White Princess continued, disappointment in her voice.

"Kou, it's fine, isn't it?"

"No, it is not! White Princess!"

He stepped behind one of the bedposts, putting distance between them so she couldn't leap at him.

Realizing her efforts weren't working, White Princess puffed up her cheeks even more, but then her expression quickly darkened. She cast her eyes down, a deep sadness in them.

Kou was struck with uncertainty. That expression was a low blow.

He really didn't want to make her look so sad.

"Um, White Princess, please don't look so disappointed."

"Aren't you lonely?"

"Lonely?"

"You are my gift, my nourishment, my master, my king, my servant, my joy, my fate, my Groom. You told me you were waiting for me. Was that a lie?"

"It wasn't a lie, but…"

"I care for you, Kou. Being separated from my fate makes me lonely."

A horribly upset look came across her face. She looked like a young child who had been abandoned. Being rejected really made White Princess feel that lonely. She pressed a hand to her chest.

In an almost singsong voice, she said, "You are my one and only. You are more precious to me than anything and more beloved than anyone. I am willing to face anything for you. But I want to be by your side. I ~~am~~ ~~from you.~~"

This broke Kou. ~~He knew~~ ~~what~~ there was a hole in your heart. That was something that Kou had felt for so long, tormented by an emptiness he had no way to fill.

…I am lonely without you.

Kou thought he would spend eternity unable to find the person he sought.

But White Princess was here with him now. And she looked lonely.

He let out a sigh and sat on the bed again. He pulled back the blanket and went to lie down next to White Princess.

Her eyes shone with joy, and a huge smile immediately grew on her face. "Kou!"

"Ah, White Princess…uh, come on."

She hugged him tight. He tried to peel her off, then stopped. Her hug was like the kind a younger sister would give to her elder brother. She nuzzled her head against him. The act was so innocent. Kou was completely unable to pull away.

Half desperate, he wrapped his arms around her back. He patted her gently, like he might do to a much younger sister.

"You're not lonely anymore, are you?" he asked.

"No, of course not! I feel so warm now—and happy, Kou," she said, complete honesty on her face. Kou smiled.

He stroked her head reassuringly and said, "That's good. I don't like you being lonely."

"I'm so…relieved…I'm…going into…sleep…mode…"

White Princess's body quickly went limp, and her breathing slowed.

Kou stroked her head again, whispering gently as he straightened her hair.

"Good night, White Princess. Sweet dreams."

He pulled his hand back, smiling, and his eyelids soon grew heavy.

* * *

In the middle of the night, Kou opened his eyes again. He looked around the room. Moonlight poured in through the window.

In that silvery light stood a woman. At first, Kou thought she was White Princess, but she wasn't.

She was wearing a black dress with silver chains sparkling around her white neck. The ends of the chains disappeared into her ample cleavage; she was utterly bewitching. She stared down at Kou where he lay in bed.

Her black hair and eyes were like the night.

Her white skin like the snow.

For some reason, Kou didn't question why she was there. Something about this felt oddly familiar. The woman, meanwhile, gazed upon Kou with such lonely eyes.

She bent over slightly, as if to peer more closely at him. Kou saw something blue sparkle by her ears from beneath her black hair. Her sorrowful expression was unchanged.

He didn't understand why she looked so lonely.

Taking care not to wake White Princess, Kou shifted over slightly to one side of the bed. He pulled back the cover and offered, "Why don't you get in, too? Look... You won't be lonely if we're close."

Her eyes opened wide, and her lips trembled. But she stubbornly shook her head.

The blue sparkled at her ears again.

She looked to be on the verge of tears as she pressed a hand to her chest and stretched the other toward Kou. Her fingers shook, clutching, yearning, but she squeezed her fist tight.

Her form rapidly began fading before she disappeared into the night.

Eventually, morning came.

When Kou opened his eyes, there were no signs that anyone had

room.

nothing behind.

"Yes?" he called.

"I know it's early in the morning...but could y

muffled voice from the other side of the thick layer of wood.

Kou tilted his head dubiously but opened the door.

Standing on the other side was a male student with bandages wrapped around his head. The boy had a unique appearance, with his single visible eye and red hair. Kou scrutinized him with narrowed eyes.

Perhaps out of consideration for Kou's unease, the boy spoke gently.

"Hey, sorry about this. Do you have a minute?"

"Sure, but...who are you?" asked Kou. He searched through his memory. He felt like he'd seen this boy's face and heard his voice somewhere.

Unconsciously, Kou thought of a conversation he had overheard in the classroom:

"Tsubaki, no killing. Kagura will murder you if you do. Or are you fine with that?"

"Be quiet, Hikami."

This must be Hikami, thought Kou.

Hikami suddenly held out a hand. A couple seconds later, Kou realized he was asking for a handshake and quickly responded. The skin on Hikami's palm was thick, with many obvious scars.

After the handshake, Hikami introduced himself again.

"My name's Ryuu Hikami. I'm a third-year student. Sorry for interfering with your exam yesterday."

"No, don't worry about it... That actually helped me. Thank you."

Kou bowed his head. He didn't know whether Tsubaki would have let her guard down if Hikami hadn't tried to stop her.

"Well, all right. If you're sure." Hikami smiled, then abruptly cleared his throat. "So then, about the second exam..."

"The second exam?"

"Due to the risk of a transfer student's kihei getting out of control, two or more students are always assigned to monitor their first night... So I saw and heard everything that happened last night. Sorry."

"Ah!" cried Kou, unable to respond with anything more eloquent. He thought back to his conversation with White Princess the night before and turned red. He couldn't help feeling the urge to cradle his head in his hands in embarrassment, but Hikami quickly continued speaking.

"No, it's okay! It's perfectly fine for a Bride and a Groom to get along! There's nothing you need to be embarrassed about. You passed the exam with flying colors. You should be proud!" insisted Hikami, even more flustered than Kou. He seemed to be the kind of person who was considerate about others' feelings.

Kou nodded after somehow managing to steady himself. "A-all right. Thank you for keeping an eye on things."

"N-no problem. I'm just glad you've calmed down... Contracts with Brides always come out of nowhere." Hikami suddenly changed the subject. His tone was heavy, as if something had happened in the past. "There's probably a lot of things that'll throw you off, but 'We are Pandemonium. Our Brides and our skills are everything.' You can relax. From what I saw in the exam, you definitely have what it takes to be here... Let's both keep working hard."

"Goodness, Hikami. It seems you've beaten me to it," came a sudden, cool voice.

Kou looked down the hallway. Behind Hikami was a graceful female student. This was Mirei, the upperclassman who'd explained things to him yesterday. Her chestnut-colored hair swayed as she looked between Hikami and Kou, a playful pout on her lips.

"I was the other person assigned to surveillance. I was hoping to tease you a little bit more, but I think it would be a rude at this point... I hope you don't mind me saying hello. Welcome again, Kou Kaguro, to Pandemonium."

She placed a hand on her ample bosom and gave a slight bow as she welcomed him.

_____ smile, she continued to say, "I welcome the strong. ____ lie in the dark. But at the

row appeared between Hikami's brow.

Observing the pair's demeanor, Kou couldn't help inquiring, don my asking, but...are you two a couple?"

"Mirei and me? Ha-ha-ha! Now, that's funny."

"That would never happen, not even if the land and the heavens were flipped upside down."

They both shook their heads in unison. They seemed so in sync that Kou was somewhat surprised they weren't a couple. He apologized for his misinterpretation, but Mirei smiled like it wasn't really a problem.

"I have no intention of considering a partner other than my Bride," she said. "But I'm stuck with Hikami. We joined Pandemonium at nearly the same time. You could say we're old acquaintances."

"We've probably only made it this far because we've relied on each other. That much is true," said Hikami.

Kou nodded in acceptance. In other words, they had a close friendship that had carried on from the time they joined Pandemonium.

With a big nod, Hikami continued.

"I'm Wasp Rank, and Mirei's Demon Rank. There's been a lot of times when her strength has saved me."

"Despite appearances, Hikami's abilities are incredibly useful. He's been given a lot of responsibilities within Pandemonium. I'm sure you will find him helpful on many occasions in the future as well."

"You're being too generous with your compliments, Mirei. So I'm the hardest working and bravest person in the classroom?"

"Ha-ha, well, no one said that."

Hikami struck a pose, and Mirei immediately shot back with a jab.

Kou felt even more keenly how connected these two were. He declared honestly, "You two really are close. I'm a bit jealous."

"You're our companion, too," said Hikami. "Don't be afraid to act like it. And yeah... I hope you find some friends in your same year, too. All right, I think we should tell you a bit about what Pandemonium usually does."

"Yes, let's," said Mirei. "Kou, first let me tell you about the cafeteria..."

With that, Hikami and Mirei taught Kou all sorts of different things: that the people in Pandemonium tended to be moody, that the food in the cafeteria was to die for, that he would start having normal classes today, and so on and so forth.

Finally, not wanting to overstay their welcome, the two left Kou's room together. Kou said good-bye and thanked them for their help.

He closed the door and stretched.

And that was the start of Kou and White Princess's life in Pandemonium.

Before the clock rang, she awoke.

incredibly gentle.

That's why she decided to slip into sleep again.

Wishing for just one more good dream.

Desiring to go meet her beloved.

The god's dream brought other changes. The darkness groaned and churned. Effected by the noble one, they had started swarming. She cared nothing for that and continued her deep, deep slumber.

The dream was peaceful.

It was happy.

And it was empty.

* * *

"…All right, so those are the types of kihei recently confirmed in the central labyrinth, the distribution map of incubation nests, and predicted trends for areas yet to be investigated. This diagram will definitely be on the test, so make sure you memorize it. Uh, none of you are actually listening, are you?"

The large classroom was filled with Kagura's voice. A small panel made from magic crystal floated above the lectern, displaying several lighted points on a map of the labyrinth. However, only a few students bothered to copy that into their notebooks.

Several people spoke up, noticeably lacking in motivation.

"I'm listening…"

"Totally heard every word…"

"It's fiiine."

"Even if I bomb all the tests, I won't fail the practical exam."

"Well, 'We are Pandemonium. Our Brides and our skills are everything'…right?" said Kagura. "It's not a problem as long as you do well in battle. But labyrinth information will help you on your missions, and the kids who do bad'll have to take extra classes! If you don't want that, make sure you memorize this… Ah, it's time already. Break!"

A bell rang, announcing break time in the classroom. Chairs immediately scraped across the floor as the students of Pandemonium stood. They kicked off their desks and rushed up the stairs, each of them aiming for the door.

"Sheesh, you're all in a hurry," griped Kagura.

Kou and White Princess went their own way.

"Let's go, White Princess."

"Yes, let's."

They had a promise to keep today.

They put away their notebooks and pens and started to move. Ahead of them awaited a sight they could have never imagined.

Three thick slabs of synthetic pâté. Onions, raspberry sauce, and pickles placed between two slices of bread. Then, a knife inserted through the center to keep it all in place, finishing off the huge, glorious tower. Last but not least were the fries arranged around it for decoration.

Not only did the food look delicious, there was also plenty of it.

Kou stood in front of the cook, his eyes darting back and forth as he said, "…Uh, Hikami, this is a bit…"

"Those are real raspberries. Exploration found them and gave us some. You should thank them," said Hikami.

"That's not what I mean. I'm not sure I have enough space in my stomach for this."

"That's what I'm saying. You're so thin, and you're physically weak, too. First things first: You need to make sure you're getting plenty to eat. Besides, I borrowed the kitchen to make all this, so just sit back, relax, and eat."

"No way, that's a scary amount of food."

"You sure say whatever rude thing is on your mind, don't you?" said Hikami, his visible right eye narrowed. But despite his words, his

with trees

speared one piece,

to be enjoying the pampering and acted like this was

Next, White Princess opened her mouth. With a large smile, Mirei fed her a piece of cake, too. Tsubaki and White Princess sat side by side, chewing their cake, and reacted in unison:

"Yummy!"

"Yummy!"

"Aw, you two are so cute," said Mirei. "Men and spouses are for teasing, but girls are for spoiling! With a flower at either side, I couldn't be happier."

Mirei displayed an exquisite smile. She brought a hand to her cheek and wriggled in delight.

Tsubaki and White Princess both asked for more cake, and Mirei kindly obliged. The three of them seemed to be having a lovely time.

Hikami, on the other hand, was practically growling at Kou.

Why is it like this? Kou wondered deep down.

The peaceful chaos continued.

Ten days had passed since Kou's battle with Tsubaki.

For some reason, since their battle, Tsubaki had been popping up around him constantly. Despite having lost, she seemed to have taken a liking to him.

On one occasion, Tsubaki stole Kou's dinner. By the time Hikami caught her, Kou's sandwich had disappeared into her mouth. An image of her cheeks bulging like a chipmunk's was still fresh in his mind. But a moment later, she leaned against Kou like a capricious kitten and fell asleep.

"*You're so laid-back, it's only right for me to give a little poke now and then,*" she would say, then pull some prank on him.

Perhaps concerned about this, Hikami and Mirei soon began accompanying them. Hikami, in particular, was always looking out for Kou, ever since he said hello that first day.

He offered Kou advice about everything from battle to life. Before long, he was even giving Kou food to improve his health, like today. If you looked at it another way, you could say that Hikami was a meddler at heart.

Lately, he had complaints about Kou's physique.

"You're quick on the uptake, and your coordination with White Princess is excellent," he said. "But you lack a good fundamental physical strength. You can enhance it, depending on how you use your magic, but in the end, it's physical strength that makes or breaks a fight. You need to eat more."

Right now, he was acting like an overbearing mother. Kou shrank back, wondering what he should do.

Mirei was neatly slicing another bit of cake. She put a piece in Tsubaki's mouth and even held a teacup up for her to take a sip. Her eyes gently turned toward Hikami, and in a mild tone, she said, "Cooking is Hikami's hobby, you know. I think he enjoys making you food. Could you forgive him?"

"Ha-ha-ha! So I'm a genius chef with a heart of gold?" asked Hikami.

"Hee-hee, no one said that," teased Mirei with a sunny smile, but that didn't stop Hikami from arrogantly brushing his hand through his bangs.

Their banter was casual and merciless but as filled with friendship as always.

Mirei cocked her head slightly, then looked at Kou and said, "So anyway. Won't you go along with it? Even if it means pushing your stomach to its limits."

"That's unreasonable," said Kou.

"We can figure something out, though, can't we?"

"No, we can't."

"No need to worry, Kou. I'll finish off everything," said White Prin-
~~~ified tone between bites of cake. Beside her sat Tsubaki,
~~~ She had so much cake packed in that

~~~cess.

~~~ Yep, ~~~

A snake-shaped kinei ~~~
its body, a mix of mechanics and muscle, ~~~
mottled pattern of red and black. It was a Type B kinei, ~~~
as impressive as a Type A.

Hikami scratched his Bride under the chin, then kissed its forehead. He snapped his fingers again, and Unknown disappeared. Kou hadn't noticed it at the time, but Hikami had been in the group of masked students who escorted Kou and White Princess when they first arrived. In fact, he was also the student whose shoulder Kagura put his hand on, before he escaped the teacher a moment later.

After seeing this display, Kou had a question.

"You really dote on your Bride, don't you, Hikami?"

"Of course, we're married… Isn't it the same with you?"

"With me?"

"From the sidelines, it seems like you spoil her quite a bit… Am I wrong?" asked Hikami, curious.

Without a moment's delay, White Princess jumped in. She pounded the table as she cried, "Hikami, that's excellent. Please tell Kou. I think he can love me at least fifty-three times his current rate, at which point I will return his love at a rate of five hundred and thirty times, and we will be very happy. It will be wonderful. There is no downside."

"See, there you have it. Treasure her more," said Hikami, sounding almost like a father as he patted Kou's shoulder.

With a sip of her own tea, Mirei was the next to speak. Her eyes appeared focused on something far in the distance as she began.

"The majority of us entered our marriage while battling a kihei or merely coming across one, and that bond is the only reason we survived. We would already be dead if not for our Brides... We owe them our lives, and they give us love, so how could we not love them back?"

Kou was somewhat surprised by Mirei's statement. So it was true—she and the others had also made contracts directly after harrowing events. At the same time, Kou fully understood Mirei's feelings. He, too, had been saved by his encounter with White Princess. That's why he was here. It seemed that Tsubaki was in a different situation, though.

She laid her head on Doll's Guardian's knee and said, "It's not quite the same for me. My father was a soldier, and when I was ten, I took on his contract. That's how Doll's Guardian and I started our lives together. Because of that, people have tried to kill me so many times."

"Kill you...? That kind of thing happens?" asked Kou in shock.

Tsubaki nodded innocently. In contrast to the gesture, her tone was flat as she continued.

"I'm sure you know how much average people fear kihei. Other than the Coexisters, of course, and those people are nuts in their own way... Anyway, I was rescued when I was taken in by the Academy. Humans scare me more than kihei. They're not cute, plus they're unpleasant and difficult to forgive... I have no interest in the fight against the kihei."

Tsubaki's words were clear and straightforward. She reached out a small hand and gently stroked Doll's Guardian's hard head. Her voice was filled with obvious affection as she said, "I'm just here so I can live my life with Doll's Guardian."

Humans had rejected Tsubaki and even tried to take her life. She was courageous for living through a life like that.

Kou stopped trying to think of something to say. Tsubaki's eyes said she didn't want any trite words of comfort. Someone as limited in life experience as Kou had nothing to add.

Instead, he conjured an image of their classroom.

Each and every one of the members of Pandemonium was close with their kihei companion. They showered love on their Brides. That set them apart from the other students.

Kou couldn't hold back his next question.

"Why do all of you fight for Pandemonium?"

"Ah, as a new member, you're curious about our reasons?" said Hikami with a strong nod. He closed his eye for a moment and ordered his thoughts. Bringing a hand to his chest, he said in a grave tone, "Because we're married to kihei, we are clearly different from your ... There's no other place for us to live. We live here, and ... and I want ... like him. ...

"I was originally a squad leader. Although... ... talk about the details. Sorry," he said, stumbling over his words. He shook his head and closed his one intact eye. He looked like he was praying.

Mirei naturally picked up where he left off. She stirred her tea as she quietly said, "To be honest, I have no interest in reducing casualties… I was orphaned when there was a conflict between my parents, who were both from prominent families. I was almost killed while on an investigation mission in the Department of Magic Research, and I was saved by my Bride."

Mirei absentmindedly stroked her chestnut-colored hair. Her eyes were clear as she told her story.

Kou reflexively clenched his fists when he heard her mention an investigation mission in the Department of Magic Research. He'd experienced a similar tragedy. There was nothing a squad of people from Research could do to fight back if they happened upon a powerful kihei.

Mirei nodded in sympathy with Kou and then said, "If My Kitty didn't love me, I would have been sliced in half… That's why the only things that matter to me are my friends and him. I will be satisfied so long as I can live a happy life with My Kitty and all of you. This is the only place we can live… That, and my resolve to fight to the death for this place and our peaceful time here, is something I share with Hikami."

That was where Mirei finished speaking. She still had a gentle smile as she stepped on her Bride. There was obvious affection on her face.

Knowing it might be rude, Kou hesitantly asked anyway, "Um, Mirei… Is there some reason you express affection for your Bride that way?"

"No, it's just a preference of mine."

"Just a preference?"

"A fetish, you might say."

"Right, got it." Kou nodded.

Ignoring the fetish thing, both of these stories had a similar courageousness to them. Kou guessed that everyone in Pandemonium had their own situations and reasons for fighting.

At the same time, Kou recalled the words he'd heard:

"We are the proud members of Pandemonium. We lie in the dark, spoken ill of by others. Our Brides and our skills are everything."

This academy was made to fight against the kihei…and this is the nonexistent class one hundred, he thought.

Pandemonium's classroom was in Central Headquarters, separate from the other students. Every single one of Pandemonium's students, including Kou, was abnormal in the Academy.

Listening to Tsubaki and the others talk, Kou felt his understanding deepen.

Before, he had been called a white mask, but now he really had become something strange and unknown, both in name and in reality. He'd been vaguely aware for some time now, but Kou realized he needed to face the truth.

I probably won't ever see Asagiri and Isumi again.

Now that he was married to a kihei, there was nowhere for him to live besides Pandemonium. But that didn't upset Kou. He was sad he wouldn't be able to see Asagiri and Isumi again, but that was probably better for them anyway. Besides, he always had White Princess by his side. She was sitting beside him, smiling.

When she was with him, he felt like the hole in his chest had been filled.

That feeling struck him suddenly. He looked at her, and she smiled back.

Unconsciously, he opened his mouth.

"White Princess."

"What is it, Kou?"

... your Groom," vowed Kou again. This deter-
... lizing

"Well, then ...
happens, I will protect you. Kou, I will be by your side, ... thing for you, for all eternity," she replied earnestly.

They looked into each other's eyes and smiled.

Beside them, Tsubaki rolled her eyes and said, "What the heck are you making us watch?"

"No, no, it's perfectly fine for a married couple to get along!" retorted Hikami with a strong nod.

Kou listened to the two of them as he squeezed White Princess's hand. He nodded, a gesture filled with emotion.

These days with White Princess really are precious, thought Kou, feeling it keenly.

And besides, his daily life in Pandemonium was going surprisingly peacefully.

Now then, he thought as he turned his gaze to the problem in front of him.

*   *   *

He carefully divided the food, pierced half of the main dish on his fork, and moved it over to White Princess. She opened her mouth wider than he would have thought possible and practically swallowed the food whole. Kou then ate the remainder himself.

Hikami deeply creased his brow and groaned.

"Hmm, at least you're eating half of it. That makes it hard to complain."

"It's delicious. Thank you, Hikami," said Kou.

"Aaaah!"

"Tsubaki, even if you open your mouth, I'm not going to put any food in it...," said Kou.

"I knew it; you are so not cute. Think about what you've done, then go die," she replied.

"You're ridiculous."

Tsubaki pouted like she didn't know what he was talking about, then moved up to Doll's Guardian's shoulder. She curled gracefully into a ball, making her look exactly like a kitten.

"Yeah, yeah," said Kou to Tsubaki as he wiped White Princess's mouth.

Their days were chaotic, but it was a tranquil chaos.

Other than battle training, of course.

* * *

"Nope, no good! No good at all!"

Kou felt like his insides would flip upside down. He gasped for breath while crawling on the floor. Taunts flew in his direction from the other students who were watching his clumsy performance.

"Weak."

"Pathetic."

"Try a bit harder."

"Go for it!"

"You can do it!"

And so on. A few of his peers were fairly kind, actually, but the general response was negative.

He listened to the jeers but remained unable to stand. Blades pierced through his hands and feet—they were none other than White Princess's own feathers pinning Kou down. This was the result of his battle training with Kagura.

Against any other person, Kou had been able to manage just as he'd done with Tsubaki, but he was defenseless against Kagura. Kou didn't even know when his weapons had been taken away from him. By the time he realized it, they were gone and pierced through all four of his limbs.

Kagura walked over, looking bored. He grabbed the feathers still stuck in Kou and then pulled them all out, one after another. Kou swallowed a scream. Kagura then cast healing magic on his wounds.

The pain faded, as did White Princess's aggression, which he had ....position behind him. She glared at Kagura.

.... We're

one, too.

Kagura stabbed Kou's left hand again. Intense ..... through his body strong enough to make his stomach churn. White Princess moved to leap in front of him, but Kou stopped her with a look.

Kagura, on the other hand, heaved a deep sigh. It seemed he wasn't torturing Kou just for kicks.

"Didn't you sense my hostility the whole time I was talking?" he said. "When I do that, I need you to dodge. And I made it so easy to see. If you keep focused and read your opponent—"

"—!"

Kagura quickly threw a blade at Kou's feet.

But this time, Kou knocked the blade away with one of his own.

There, other students stirred. Kagura grinned. Kou followed up by throwing his blade at Kagura's face. Kagura caught the blade between two fingers and nodded slightly.

"Guess that'll do for a start. Let's wrap it up there. Okay, White

Princess, you can move now! You can even attack me if you like! I'll return it all in kind, though."

"White Princess, we're done! Come here," called Kou. White Princess immediately rushed to him, slipping into his arms. Kou patted her back, calming her down.

"Kou, I'm unhappy. I'm unhappy standing by and watching you get hurt. I'm supposed to be your wings!"

"Thank you for worrying about me, but I'm okay. Don't be so angry."

She growled, and he gently stroked her head, causing her to bounce up and down with joy. It was such a genuine reaction.

Kou softly said, "You're so good, White Princess."

"Kou, more. You should show your love more, then I will return even more love."

"Okay, okay."

White Princess bounced even more. He stroked her head. These sorts of physical displays of affection had quickly become part of their everyday life. He would stroke her head, hold her hand, hug her, wipe her mouth.

They were constantly glued to each other, like they were the other's only family. And ever since that first night, they always slept while cuddling one another.

White Princess smiled, and Kou mused, *When I first heard we were married, I was so hesitant.*

But at this point, Kou felt like it was only natural that White Princess was by his side. Her warmth was comforting. The space she filled would surely be so empty if she was gone. He couldn't help feeling this way.

Those indistinct memories of someone innocent and childlike—Kou had begun to wonder if that someone was her.

I've had these vague memories for as long as I can remember...so there's no way it could be White Princess; I only just met her recently...but I also can't help feeling that it couldn't be anyone but her.

The only time Kou's strange emptiness felt filled was when he was with White Princess. That was a precious feeling. He didn't think there was anyone else who could fill that hole in him.

Even now, she clung to his arm. Yet her voice was filled with frustration again as she said, "But you know, I cannot let him get away with hurting you as he wishes. I'd like to bash him over the head at least once with my wing... Grrrrr!"

"We'd lose that fight, though, so just calm down. There, there."

White Princess still looked angry. Kou tickled her chin and tried to calm her. She continued to growl, but her mouth began to form a smile once again.

That's when Kagura suddenly clapped his hands together. Usually, he'd leave immediately after battle training was over. Today, however, he circled around to the back of the lectern and raised his voice. All eyes gathered on him.

"All right, attention, everybody! Hey, don't look away. Don't talk to the kid next to you; hey there!" he said.

lectern, looking

All of a sudden, his attitude shifted.

In a complete change, his voice turned cold and calculating. "Contact has been lost with the Department of Exploration's Deep Expedition Team," he said. "It's a team comprised of only sixth-year veteran students. Even a Combat team would have trouble following after them. That's why a search request has been sent over to Pandemonium."

His hollow voice filled the room. The students' attitudes immediately changed as well. They started asking serious questions, as if that was how they always were.

"Where were they and what was the exploration target?"

"Zone Seven in the central labyrinth, a dangerous area with Type A kihei," replied Kagura. "They were in the process of developing a safe route for exploration, but it seems they made an error in judgment. This is an emergency, but it always is. As is customary, I'm going to ask our newbies to join the mission. White Princess, Kou—I'm sure you're fine with that, yes?"

"Huh?" Kou was at a loss for words as he pointed to himself.

"It's a search and rescue. Either that or a body recovery. I'll also be sending some of the students you've gotten familiar with—and another who's only been out once before. Always uphold Pandemonium's pride."

This order came out of nowhere.

Kou had always stayed near the surface of the prehistoric ruins, excluding the time he fell into the hole. Refusing the order didn't seem like an option, though. That much was clear from Kagura's eyes.

White Princess must have sensed Kou's unease, because she cheerfully said, "It's okay, Kou. I will always be with you... And it sounds like Tsubaki and the others will be coming, too. We should be able to manage."

"'Human lives are worth little, but the trust you can gain is worth much.' There is a high likelihood that they're already dead, but they'll owe us a favor if you can save them. Do your best. Well, then..."

Kagura gave a disconcerting smile.

Tsubaki, Hikami, and Mirei stood as if that were some sort of signal. Another person stood as well, likely the second-timer Kagura had mentioned. He was a male student, his mouth covered by a scarf.

They all stood at the ready.

Kagura clapped his hands together and spoke again, as if he were announcing the opening act of a play.

"And now begins your first mission."

The Bride of Demise

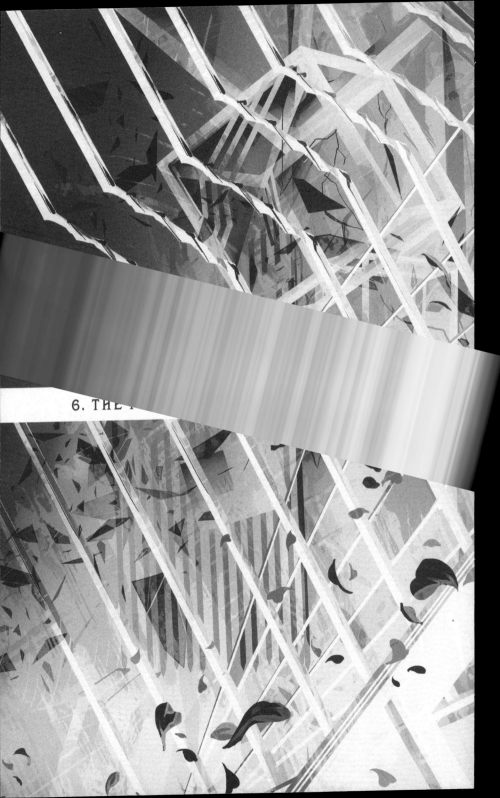

The god's dreams had

The darkness groaned and churned—and expanded.

Numerous kihei marched forward. Forward. Forward. Forward. Forward. Forward.

They became a horrific horde.

They sought the one she so wanted to meet.

Yet she still didn't open her eyes.

The darkness roared.

And she slept.

* * *

There were still many mysteries concealed within the prehistoric ruins.

Even so, investigations had made significant progress in several of them. The large-scale ruins known as the central labyrinth were particularly full of valuable relics, and the Department of Exploration was making concentrated efforts to bring the area under control.

The most well-known goal of Exploration was to uncover relics, but their more important responsibility was to scout out points they believed could be cleared out. Exploration was constantly patrolling the ruins and reporting information to Combat about locations they thought could be turned into Clean Zones. This, in turn, provided locations with a guaranteed level of safety, expanding footholds within the ruins for further expeditions.

But even a tiny miscalculation could lead to immediate death.

The Department of Exploration was overflowing with dreams of the unknown, but its casualty rate was second only to the Department of Combat.

In the ruins, in the region outside the Academy's walls, people died without reason.

Just like the corpses collapsed on the ground in front of Kou Kaguro and the others now.

The results of their first mission had already come in.

They were too late.

Hikami and Mirei spoke calmly in the face of this hellish scene.

"Looks like we were too late," said Hikami. "And they were played with. You get used to it, but it's not a pleasant sight no matter how many times you see it."

"No point in feeling sorry for them if they were already dead when it happened," said Mirei. "They wouldn't have felt any pain."

"…Looks like it's been more than a day since they died. Meaning it was all over before we even got the search request…," said the student with the scarf over his face as he crouched by the bodies. Those words brought Kou an iota of relief. It wasn't that they were too late; there was already no way of saving them by the time they left for the mission.

But that doesn't change the fact that people died, he thought.

"…Worrying about it is wasted time. That's what I think," said the boy without looking in Kou's direction. It didn't seem like he was trying to make Kou feel better, nor did it seem like he was talking to himself. Kou still hadn't asked his name, though he knew he was a Wasp Rank. His hair was black and long. Even with the lower half of his face hidden beneath a scarf, Kou could tell that he had attractive, androgynous features.

The boy placed a decomposing arm back on the ground. Fragments of bodies littered the area around them. Everything was sliced into small bits, including the magic armor.

By Kou's feet were pieces of flesh with bone sticking out and a frag-
~~nt of jaw, the teeth still in a row, though the tongue and other
~~~~ out. It looked like the situation here was very similar to
~~~~~ Research students had run into that Special

~~~~~~ mains.

help the ~~~
ing have obligations. ~

"Yeah, I get it… I just wish we ~~
had to push ourselves," replied Kou.

"Are you a moron?" said Tsubaki. "They were dead w~
still chatting in the classroom. It's moronic to talk about something impossible…which makes you a moron."

Her voice was as cute as ever as she spoke, but her face was expressionless. By now, Kou had come to understand that this was her way of showing she cared. Not that she liked being thanked for it.

Kou just nodded in agreement. She was right, and he was fine with being a moron.

He crouched low to the ground. It would be impossible to gather all the fragments of the remains with how chopped up they were. He also couldn't bear the thought of the different bodies becoming even more mixed together as they carried them back.

As he'd been ordered to do earlier, he looked for fragments with magic armor that showed the owner's identification number, then he packaged together the pieces of bone and flesh that he thought belonged to the same person. He carefully placed each and every one in the boxes. Despite his words, even he noticed that he appeared relatively unaffected.

Mirei glanced at him and nodded, looking relieved. It seemed she'd been worried he'd taken an emotional hit.

Kou continued the work in silence. The other boy crouched beside him. He pulled down the scarf around his face and, in a muffled voice, whispered, "...I'll help... The remains in your area are pretty badly damaged."

"Thank you... May I ask your name?" said Kou.

"We're in the same year; you don't have to be so formal... And I don't think my name's necessary for doing the job."

He readjusted the scarf and began gathering the bones around him. His gray eyes were cold and calm. Kou didn't know what to say. He placed a left arm and armor fragment in a clear bag.

Then he said, "If I don't know your name, it could slow down communication during battle... A moment's hesitation could mean life or death... Don't you think?"

"There's some logic to that... I'm Rui Yaguruma... I'd prefer you call me Yaguruma."

"All right then, Yaguruma. Thanks for helping me...and for what you said earlier."

"You can thank me by working quickly."

"I think it's necessary to say it."

"...Yeah, and I'd be the moron if I rejected it," said Yaguruma, his expression never changing. Kou was relieved they were able to talk.

Their surroundings were horrific, but even in the current situation, making more acquaintances in Pandemonium sounded like a good plan. In the ruins, in particular, your life depended on these people.

Everyone else was hard at work as well. Not just Hikami and Mirei, but even Tsubaki was carefully packaging up the corpses. Every once in a while she would snort, but she also closed her jade eyes many times as if in prayer.

For a while, they passed the time in silence. And finally, they finished gathering the right amount of remains for the members of the Expedition squad. All they could do now was pray they weren't wrong.

While they were working, White Princess had been walking aimlessly around the area. She had no interest in or concern about the death of people she didn't know. Kou felt he was seeing a kihei-like aspect of her character for the first time.

Kou and the others finished packing away the bags of remains. As Yaguruma closed a box, he muttered, "…The death of veteran explorers like them is a serious blow. I hope we can kill all the kihei as soon as possible."

"Huh?" replied Kou without thinking. Those words were unexpected. True, the scene in front of them was gruesome. The dead would never return, and many would mourn. But to Pandemonium, the kihei were also allies.

Or so he had thought. Ever since Kou had heard that White Princess ... humanity's enemy. Appar-

lot of those in Pandemonium....

Yaguruma shrugged and buried the bottom half of his face into his scarf. What he said wasn't very characteristic of someone from their class. Then something struck Kou. This was Yaguruma's second mission. He was probably the other transfer student Mirei had talked about.

Among the regular students, there were many who loathed the kihei. But even before Kou had made his contract with White Princess, he hadn't entirely decided how he felt about the subject. It was possible that Isumi had sensed this indecision, and that was one of the reasons he was angry with Kou.

For one thing, Kou's parents had been killed by humans, not kihei.

That was part of the reason why he chose to go into the Department of Magic Research. He wanted to know more about these creatures that were considered humanity's enemy. And he wanted to confirm if it was true that kihei, rather than humans, were the more terrifying of the two.

That and, for some reason, he felt he had to learn more about them.

...I felt as if it were my life's duty.

Kou tried to put this obscure urge into words, but he didn't have the time to.

Hikami swiftly raised an arm, let out an energized shout, and gave the order.

"All right, we're going back, everyone. Things went well on the way here, but that's no guarantee it'll be the same on the way back. Death can smile upon you at any time. Keep on your toes."

Everyone nodded back. Kou put a box filled with remains on his back.

The dark path through the central labyrinth stretched out ahead of them.

* * *

Fortunately, the road itself was obvious, because Exploration had left behind a map. Except they hadn't. There was no map.

It was thanks to the ability of Hikami's Unknown.

"All right, my beloved wife. Dazzle us with your power!"

Unknown split into eight slender pieces in response to Hikami's order, and each of the pieces disappeared. Unknown proceeded to scout out the area beyond. Hikami pressed a hand to his head. Then, after some time, he muttered, "Routes one, two, four, and six are no good...and a Type A's appeared on the route we used to come here. That leaves three, five, seven, eight... Eight is the best out of those. Let's go."

"Hikami may only be a Wasp Rank, but on usefulness alone, he far surpasses Demon Rank, don't you think?" said Mirei.

"Ha-ha-ha! So I'm a hard worker who has perfect coordination with my Bride?"

"Hee-hee, no one said that."

They fell into the same type of exchange as always. Once that was over, they started out again.

Inside the ruins, it was dark, but there were walls that gave off light at regular intervals. They were likely made of the same material as the confinement room Kou had been put in. He didn't understand how they worked, but it did mean they didn't have to use their own lights.

Doll's Guardian headed the group, acting as a shield.

Hikami's scouting paid off. They were left in peaceful silence for a while.

That is, until Doll's Guardian suddenly stopped walking. The others followed his lead and held their breath.

Doll's Guardian created a massive wall in front of himself. There was a *brat-a-tat-tat*, and multiple sharp objects pierced into the barrier. The wall protected them against the attack, leaving hundreds of spines stuck in it.

was ahead using Unknown. Then he clicked

It wasn't there

Kitty is

his chain with a jangling sound.

The kihei wrapped in those chains stumbled forward. He looked very unsteady, but Mirei snapped her fingers without hesitation.

With a clear voice overflowing with trust, she ordered, "You may undo your binding, my beloved. Show me your true, beautiful form."

Mirei's Bride trembled slightly. The chains fell from his body with a rattle as his strange form changed. The membrane-like substance that appeared to cover his humanoid body disappeared.

Kou's eyes widened in surprise.

Out from the membrane stepped a human. He was an attractive man with blue hair, and his slender frame suited his kind-looking facial features. He gave off the impression of an intelligent, lively young person, except that his eyes, legs, and arms were mechanical. Kou knew this wasn't technically a "person." It was beautifully constructed, but it was a kihei, a Full Humanoid.

"So Mirei's Bride isn't a Special Type?" whispered Kou.

"Nope, her companion is a Full Humanoid," said Hikami.

Doll's Guardian stood to the side, while My Kitty ran forward gracefully. He was so fast it was hard to believe how unsteady he'd been only seconds before.

"He's stronger than most Special Types," Hikami added.

Kou looked down the hallway where he could see a Special Type kihei vaguely shaped like a human, spines growing out of every inch of its body. My Kitty and the kihei stood face-to-face, stopped for just a moment.

My Kitty's legs tensed, and the surface of the enemy kihei's body ballooned.

All at once, hundreds of spines launched through the air. It was the same attack that Doll's Guardian had blocked earlier.

Her face expressionless, Mirei murmured, "…Set."

My Kitty immediately kicked up the chains around his feet and spun them skillfully in the air. Every single one of the spines was knocked aside by the chains. He picked up one spine that had clattered to the ground near him, then kicked off again. My Kitty leaped all the way up to the ceiling in what looked like a dance, then began a descent from midair.

Her expression unmoving, Mirei murmured, "…End it."

My Kitty landed on the kihei's head and forced the spine through its skull. Still holding on to the spine, he tilted his body weight forward. There was a horrific, earsplitting rending sound as My Kitty tore vertically through the kihei's internal structures.

Kou gaped. That was not your average level of skill.

After several convulsions, the Special Type kihei stilled. The mutilated corpse collapsed to the ground, more than half its face mangled.

At the same time, My Kitty's body went limp. The membrane reappeared and wrapped itself around his body. The chains moved of their own accord, binding him tight. He had returned to his former shape, a chain-bound humanoid.

Mirei ran over to her Bride. She wrapped her arms around him, like an innocent little girl. Now that he was done fighting, she showered him with passionate kisses.

"He's so incredible, isn't he? Don't you think? It's because he usually restrains himself that he's so graceful while in Full Humanoid form. As expected from the one who loves me. My dearly, dearly beloved."

"As amazing as always. Now, let's get going... Actually, wait. What is that...?" asked Hikami as he came to a dead halt.

"Yes. You noticed as well, Hikami?" said White Princess. Kou, the box of remains still on his back, looked at her questioningly. Her beautiful blue eyes looked ahead.

Catching darkness on the surface of her eyes, she said, "Hikami, I'd like you to lead us to a wide-open space. This time, it's my turn."

"Yeah, hold on... The route the third one went down looks suitable. This way. Hurry."

"_____?" asked Kou uneasily, but no one responded.

_____. She pulled him

A troop...

of working in a group..."

"Not normally, no. I'm aware of that, too. But it's the truth. And they number..."

White Princess sped up. Kou stumbled and started to fall. White Princess grabbed him from the side, and then she lifted him, like a knight might lift a princess. She continued speaking as she rushed headlong.

"...approximately one hundred."

Kou was hit with a wave of light-headedness. Even the Department of Combat would be completely wiped out with those numbers.

Whether he liked it or not, Kou was coming to a realization.

Something was happening in these ruins—something impossible.

* * *

Midway through, their mission had changed from a rescue to an escape.

Numerous Type As and Special Types were coming from behind.

With legs more powerful than a human's, they ran across the stone walls, though their attacks were blocked by Doll's Guardian. He created wall after wall behind Kou and the others, completely cutting off the bullets and blades.

Flames exploded and streamed away behind them.

They continued like that until they burst into a massive open space. Black birds took to the air. Kou's eyes widened. The light of the sun was visible here. He looked up to see an open shaft through all seven floors above them and leading to the surface. That was likely why there were so many plants growing there. The ground around them was coated in green. He wasn't sure why such a space had been dug out, but there was even a set of stairs running up along the wall, though it was half collapsed. Hundreds of birds made their nests on the rubble, and black feathers floated gently to the ground.

White Princess looked back, still holding Kou as if he was the most precious thing in the world.

Her mechanical wings shone with a gold light.

"—Hah!"

She swiped her wings at the kihei that burst into the room, turning a Type A into scrap metal. She continued to protect Kou as if he were a damsel in distress as she slaughtered the kihei, but yet another climbed over their corpses and approached.

Kihei poured from the other entrances into the space as well. They could even see a few more appearing at the top of the shaft.

Mirei and Tsubaki looked grave as they turned to the enemy and hurled orders toward their Brides.

"Protect me no matter what, Doll's Guardian!"

"Shower me with affection, My Kitty!"

The two kihei did as their Grooms commanded. The giant held fast in his position, despite multiple opponents. Numerous walls appeared. Spines and shells struck them, exploding. Doll's Guardian then began to move the walls, crushing multiple kihei in one blow. Organic matter flew into the air in all directions.

My Kitty slipped through the gaps in the kihei horde like a fencer. With elegant movements, he sliced leg after leg from the kiheis' bodies or crushed in their skulls. But it wasn't enough to thin the herd.

Unknown's role was to guide, so Hikami ordered her to fall back to a safe location. Below his eye bandages, he grimaced.

"What's going on? There aren't many reports of this sort of group appearing even in Combat's database. What's making them act together?"

"What indeed…? I think we might be in trouble… I'll call her," mur-
___. He pulled down the scarf over his mouth, showing
___ With words filled with obvious devotion, he
___ one in this world to receive my
___!"
___ hallway.

It was ___
crimson flames. ___
been following them at a distan___
enemy, a trail of flames in her wake. Organ___
ing the air with a complex mixture of smells.

But that still wasn't enough.

This horde of a hundred mostly Type A and Special Type kihei wasn't something to be taken lightly.

There's a limit to the number each Bride can handle… They'll likely crush us in the end, thought Kou, calmly judging the situation even as the encircling noose of kihei tightened around them.

The space they could stand in was being slowly eaten away. Eventually, they were driven to a small gap in the crowd at the center of the shaft. The area around them was brimming with kihei of all shapes and sizes. They were like a swarm of ants, and Kou and the others like a sugar cube placed before them.

Now it was just a matter of waiting until they were torn to shreds.

"Keep building walls until the end, Doll's Guardian!" cried Tsubaki, creating stone wall after stone wall, successfully making a pocket of safety for the moment.

Hikami and Mirei made Kou and Yaguruma fall back. The two upperclassmen chose to stand in the line of fire. Kou was a higher rank, but it seemed Hikami and Mirei had a policy of protecting underclassmen regardless of such things.

As they fell back, Hikami crossed his arms and calmly proposed a question to White Princess.

"Right, it seemed like you had an idea… What are you going to do?"

"I will…," she murmured. She turned to Kou but seemed to hesitate. She looked at the kihei surrounding them. Each of the Brides was giving it everything they had, but they were nearing their limits.

They had very little free time left.

She made her decision and nodded.

* * *

"…Kou, I have a request."

"What is it?"

"I want your blood."

Kou blinked at the sudden appeal. It didn't seem appropriate for their current situation.

He opened his mouth, then closed it. He looked at her again to judge her state of mind. She stared back at him. Her blue eyes were calm, though she narrowed them slightly.

Looking troubled, she continued before he could say anything.

"I just—I want to do something about this situation, but I feel as if there's something *incomplete* in me. I have the feeling that hole will be temporarily filled if I receive your blood…like when I first awoke," she said, clenching her fists. Her words were vague, but her resolution was firm. Even so, she shook her head in a panic and added, "I understand if you find it unpleasant, so—"

"You can have it."

"Really?"

"Of course. If you wanted it, I would give you my everything."

The words just slipped from Kou's mouth. He thought it was strange, but no matter how hard he searched through his emotions, that was truly how he felt. There was not a single trace of falsehood in it.

White Princess was always saying that she gave her wings and her being to him. He wanted to give something back, but that wasn't the only reason.

Ah... White Princess is the only thing I have, realized Kou. He thought back to everything that had happened.

Before he even knew it, his parents were dead, yet he never cried, not even when he was alone. Even when he was a kid, there were always whispers behind his back about how odd he was. The adults called him creepy.

At the Academy, he stood out from the others so much that they started calling him a white mask.

Kou Kaguro had few strong emotions. And there was no one by his side.

that wasn't entirely true.

coming closer to Hikami,

The other members of Pandemonium

own Bride was special. They were beloved, sweet, dear, precious.

Maybe even more than their own lives.

That was why the words so naturally bubbled up from Kou's throat.

"I give you my trust, my adoration, my fate. This I swear, White Princess: I will protect you for your sake."

He made his vow. Without hesitation, he bit into his finger, releasing a drop of blood. He brought his finger to her lips, and she accepted it. Her tongue licked the red up, as if following a kiss.

Her mechanical wings exploded open. Metallic arms rushed greedily through the air. An electronic sound whined, culminating in a high-pitched screech of joy.

Light and something else leaped through the space between her spread wings. Inside were not blue lines, but black.

Kou's eyes widened. This black darkness was completely different from the blue light she'd emitted before.

It devoured every inch of their surroundings, crawling over the heads of all the kihei.

They were cut down, one after another, in a chain of explosions.

It was an intense, wide-range attack.

Mirei's, Tsubaki's, and Yaguruma's Brides continued to drive back the waves of kihei, all while avoiding White Princess's attack. In the end, though, their Brides slowed to a stop.

"Incredible…," Hikami whispered tensely.

"Yes, yes, it is," murmured Mirei in the same tone.

White Princess's onslaught was simply overwhelming. She stamped out all the kihei without ever moving from her spot.

In the middle of all that stood Kou. A question came to mind for the first time.

What is the Princess Series…? And what did they mean by "the previously unconfirmed seventh member"…?

Eventually, the blood's effect wore off. White Princess stopped attacking. The blackness, which had assumed the shape of wings, scattered into the air.

More than a hundred kihei corpses had crumpled to the ground.

The Bride of Demise

She sat up, ⸺
time of no particular importance. The fated day ⸺
despite all of that, at last, she chose to stand.

The closer the fated day came, the less she could move. Now was the only time to fulfill her desires, even if only a little.

Just as she began to move, a fish-shaped kihei fell beside her and cried, "Her Highness is departing! Her Highness is departing! Her Highness is—!"

"Shut up."

She snapped her fingers and destroyed the kihei, but the commotion spread rapidly.

Thousands of kihei churned in the darkness around her.

Her Highness is departing, Her Honor is departing.

She walked among cheers of joy.

Indifference weighed heavy in her black eyes, but her footsteps were light.

As light as those of one going to see their beloved for the first time in a thousand years.

* * *

"The Princess Series is a group of kihei boasting superior power, compared even to other Full Humanoid types. They are special... They were supposedly developed during prehistoric times for use in war."

Kagura had responded readily to Kou's question. Surprisingly, it didn't appear to be confidential information. Kagura actually seemed to find it odd that Kou hadn't asked earlier.

With a furrow between his brows, Kou repeated back the information he heard.

"...A prehistoric war?"

"Yeah, that's just the Princess Series, though. We don't know if that's true about the other kihei as well. But it's fairly likely they're all prehistoric weapons. At least, that's the hypothesis the bigwigs are going with."

Kou blinked as he listened to this information. This was the first time any light had been shone onto the mystery of the kihei, although the information was nothing more than a theory.

And even if it was true, it didn't change the current situation.

If they didn't fight, they would die.

Kagura continued on with their discussion.

"So then, as for those with Princess Series Brides..."

It was break time now. The various members of Pandemonium were relaxing however they liked in the classroom. Hikami was dominating a few of their classmates in a board game. Mirei had her feet up on her Bride while she read a book. Tsubaki was curled up gracefully on Doll's Guardian's shoulder, sleeping. Yaguruma had his head down on his desk, one arm hanging limply to the side.

Kagura tapped the lectern with a finger, strumming out a little tune as he continued.

"Right now, we've got two teachers in contracts with a Princess, then when it comes to the students, there's Sasanoe. That's it. We were able to confirm six Princesses in total, based on information they provided us, but the fifth was destroyed, making her a permanent 'lost number'... Oh, by the way, this is all confidential, so you know."

"This was confidential?" asked Kou.

"Everyone in Pandemonium knows that."

"Your definition of confidential is a bit loose."

Kagura was the same as always. He just gave an easygoing shrug in response.

But his expression quickly changed. In a serious, low voice he said, "Well, you two should probably know this stuff... Considering she's the previously unconfirmed seventh Princess, and you're her Groom. And then there's her alias, Curtain Call."

Kou sucked in his breath as a realization hit him. That meant no one in the world knew anything else about White Princess. Kagura stared at the two of them, like he was sizing them up.

_____ ___ her troubling alias Curtain Call, the fact that Kou _____ _ _____ the higher-ups

...

you two."

His eyes were serious. Kou could tell he wasn't lying.

Kou thought back to his first exchange with Kagura. At the time, it had felt like he was just screwing around, but in reality, Kou's and White Princess's lives had hung in the balance.

Kagura tapped the lectern, then went on in that same icy tone, "But 'dealing' with White Princess is as difficult as it gets. It'd be easy if I took care of it, but I can't be allowed to act right now. Besides, we want as much power as we can get. To prepare for that *one in a million exception*, you know... That's why I worked so hard to get you two assigned to me. But strange things have started happening... You know what I'm talking about?"

"...The horde of kihei from the other day?" said Kou.

"Exactly. Typically, they're nothing more than automatic killing machines. They can't form 'squads.' I think their goal in joining together was to go after you. I figure that means it might be time."

"Time? Time for what?" asked Kou, but Kagura didn't answer. His blue and black eyes just creased in a smile.

Silence fell between them for a moment.

In the distance, Hikami was pointing out his seventh challenger's mistakes. Mirei shifted her feet and continued reading. Tsubaki almost slid off Doll's Guardian's shoulder, but he gently held her up with a huge hand. Yaguruma twitched in his sleep, then stilled again.

Finally, Kagura put on an ominous expression as he proposed, "That's why I'm going to have you focus on making Clean Zones for a while. The sooner after an unusual occurrence, the better. Your usual team members will join you."

"Wait a minute. I don't want to get Hikami, Mirei, Tsubaki, or Yaguruma dragged into this. If something like last time was to happen again, we may have casualties," Kou replied immediately.

White Princess managed to destroy more than a hundred kihei, using every ounce of power she had, but there was no guarantee it would go that well next time. It would be a completely different story if, instead of a horde of Type As and Special Types, it was a horde of Special Types and Full Humanoids. If that was to happen, they might even be wiped out right away.

Kou's gaze didn't waver or retreat as he stared back at Kagura.

He couldn't put the others in harm's way because of him.

But Kagura held up a palm, like he'd seen this coming. Without giving Kou a choice, he said, "It'll be fine. It's not like I want to lose students, either. That's why I'm providing you with an ace."

Kagura once again showed his disconcerting smile. It must have been meant to reassure, but it only made Kou uneasy.

"…I'm going to have Sasanoe go with you."

To Kagura, it seemed, these were the best possible conditions. He wouldn't listen to any further arguments.

Once a teacher gave their orders, students had to follow them.

And so, Kou and the others went back into the ruins.

* * *

Making a Clean Zone was incredibly simple.

You eliminated any kihei operating nearby and destroyed any incubation nests. That was it.

Incubation nests were pieces of equipment that propagated kihei. They were translucent and vaguely resembled a human womb. Each one was set into a honeycomb-shaped case, and the insides were filled with a nurturing fluid. Kihei would regularly deconstruct their own bodies and place the parts in the nest, which would allow new kihei to be born.

Students had a responsibility to destroy incubation nests on sight and gather a sample from them if possible.

using the incubation nests was incredibly hard.

scratch it, and that was

At this rate, he

Kou couldn't help thinking it.

It seemed that Sasanoe himself was well aware that other humans.

Even though they were on a mission with only members of Pandemonium, he still wore his crow mask. He didn't seem to have any intention of showing Kou and the others his real face. That appearance alone was enough to make him seem more like a kind of spirit than a human.

And then there was the beautiful kihei always by his side.

Sasanoe's Bride was the third in the Princess Series: Crimson Princess.

She had wings of silver fluid, red eyes, and hair like flames. Her clothing was a military uniform that matched her Groom's. There were no modifications or decorations to it, but the usual vermilion on both their uniforms had been changed to black.

Looking like two grim reapers, they crushed and destroyed their enemies. Kou and the others merely walked along behind them.

And as they walked, of course, they encountered kihei.

This time, too, Special Types appeared before them. There were three of them in a line, each wrapped in a smooth veil. Kou's eyes widened. This was an unlucky situation. But Sasanoe was on another level.

He didn't even need to give orders to his Bride.

He ran toward the two kihei in the back. Kou wasn't sure if he was doing it to give the others practice, but he always left one when they ran into multiple enemies. Kou and the others started to move. First, Doll's Guardian made a wall.

"Protect me, Doll's Guardian!"

"My Kitty will go first. Then White Princess…"

By the time they'd gotten that far, Sasanoe had already finished his part.

Without a word, he'd drawn the slender sword hanging at his hip. What came from the sheath wasn't metal, but a feather made of silver fluid. He took one step, swung the sword, then immediately returned the fluid to the sheath.

That was all it took.

The two Special Types were split apart, beyond recovery.

It wasn't the kind of attack a human should be capable of.

"…As amazing as always. Oh!" said Mirei, her order delayed because she had been watching Sasanoe.

The remaining Special Type morphed and evaded My Kitty's kick, but there was no need for White Princess to fire off her blue light. The Special Type was cut down in the blink of an eye. Sasanoe slid his sword back into its sheath, not saying a word.

The three corpses collapsed to the ground.

For Kou, Sasanoe's exceptional skill was now beyond question.

"Ummm, sorry, Sasanoe. And thanks, again," said Kou with a bow of his head.

"……"

The only response was silence.

Mirei and the others made no attempt to say anything, perhaps already familiar with his character.

As their exploration progressed, Sasanoe continued to refuse all interaction. Apparently, he usually created Clean Zones on his own. He and

Crimson Princess would annihilate Special Types and Full Humanoids alike.

Kou guessed he didn't like to converse with others.

Tsubaki confirmed it from where she was hanging out on Doll's Guardian's shoulder.

"There's no point, Kou. Sasanoe never talks. I once drew kitty whiskers on his face, but he didn't even react. He should have been a little surprised at least. It's totally uncute otherwise. Cats are cute, but Sasanoe is uncute. Don't you agree?"

"That sounds really dangerous," said Kou.

"Even I'm shocked! You need to stop! For the love of all that's good, stop it!" shouted Hikami. Kou's eyes met his, and Kou nodded. Tsu-

and looked like a kitten trying to be

them.

It looks like today will end without incident, too, folded the map and slid it into his inside pocket. White Princess was beside him.

She had seemed to be in a bad mood since they started this expedition. And there was a reason for that.

At first, White Princess had tried to have a friendly conversation with Crimson Princess, but Crimson Princess refused. She might not even have a voice function. Either that or she was ignoring White Princess.

White Princess apparently decided it was the latter, because she'd been silent and grumpy ever since.

Kou gently stroked her face, then walked away, but his arm was tugged back. He cocked his head and looked back to see something unexpected.

Her blue eyes shone fiercely.

She was staring ahead ominously.

Kou gulped. He tried to ask her what was wrong, but she spoke first.

"Kou…it's coming."

"Coming? Like that mixed horde from before?"

"No, no, no, not that! I…I know this…but no! I don't! I don't know anything! What is this…? What—what could it be?"

Her body shook violently. She took a step back out of fear. Her eyes stared down the path right past Sasanoe. Currently, there were no signs of anything up ahead.

But White Princess raised her voice and yelled.

"What the hell are they?!"

The next moment: *bonggggggggggggg*.

The sound of instruments resounded from the darkness.

* * *

Instruments blared.

Petals fell.

Pink and red and black and white and gold and silver.

Magnificently.

Gracefully.

Gloriously, the colors fell.

Bong, bong, the bells rang.

Between the chimes came the *huff, huff* of breathing.

A flag swayed high in the air. It was red, with some meaningless scribble resembling a crest. Below the flag were marching kihei. Beast shaped, frog shaped, fish shaped, insect shaped, human shaped, all different kinds marching at their own pace. Each lifted a leg in their own way and turned.

Then they set their backs to the walls in rows.

Kou felt dizzy.

Their movements were so human.

All the kihei raised their voices at once.

"Her Highness is arriving, Her Highness is arriving, Her Highness is arriiiiiiiiiiiiiiiiiiiiiiiving!"

The metallic declaration rent the air.

A circle was broken into the ceiling. The sun's light poured in a circular shape far down into the underground, but it was immediately swallowed by black.

A curtain of darkness fell. The chains binding the wings came undone midway and faded. Then the pitch-black wings snapped open.

Black feathers fell.

Silently. Quietly. Like the snow.

Hundreds, thousands of feathers piled in the area.

Something landed in the center with a gentle thump.

The black-and-white being raised its face.

She was a beautiful young woman.

Her black hair and eyes were like the night. Her white skin like the snow.

She was wearing a black dress of intricate design, silver chains sparkling around her neck. The ends of the chains disappeared into her full _____ body was youthful and blossoming, but her

...But that was ...

He shook his head and kept from letting his g___ idea why this woman was surrounded by kihei. But suddenly, Sasanoe's mouth opened. For the first time, words bubbled up from his lips.

"…Millennium Black Princess."

He spoke her name.

The black-and-white woman blinked. Sasanoe hunkered down like a beast about to pounce.

Then he said:

"I never thought that here, of all places, I'd get an audience with the queen of the kihei."

* * *

"…The queen of the kihei?" repeated Kou in his bewilderment. This was the first time he'd ever heard of such a thing. But there wasn't any time to ask about it now.

The next moment, someone had grabbed Kou by the collar, and he was dragged violently backward. He looked over his shoulder to see Mirei, who, with surprisingly impressive upper body strength, was now running full tilt with both Kou and White Princess in tow.

She slipped behind Doll's Guardian, who acted as a shield, completing Kou's forced evacuation.

Then came a swarm of angry voices. Throwing her gentle tone to the wind, Mirei shouted, "What are you two doing?! Isn't it obvious that battle's about to start?! This is a completely different kind of opponent from all the kihei we've fought before! You'll either get dragged into the fight or end up in the way!"

"I'm sorry, Mirei! Getting in the way would definitely be a problem! And I don't want White Princess dragged into this, either."

"Both options would be a problem, you blockhead! And you think we'd just let you go in there?!" added Hikami.

"You're right! I'm sorry!"

"I knew you were a moron, Kou! Moron!" shouted Tsubaki.

"Yes! I'm a moron!"

"…I can't cover you. Besides, it's only common sense to value your life," said Yaguruma.

"I completely agree!"

They were all angry at him, and he had no way of disagreeing with what they said. He shrank back, feeling ashamed. While everyone was yelling, White Princess was oddly quiet.

He glanced at her and saw that she was faintly trembling. He didn't know why, but she looked far more frightened than he'd ever seen her. Her blue eyes shone. She shook her head, over and over.

"…I know… No, I don't. I don't. It's so frightening, so, so…"

Kou hugged her slender shoulders tightly, trying to help her as much as he could.

He tried to tell her everything was going to be okay, but someone spoke first.

"Interesting. Amusing. How long has it been? Everything had begun to bore me. Finally," whispered Sasanoe as he drew his sword. The silver fluid caught the sun's light and gleamed brilliantly.

The moment he drew his blade, he'd already finished a series of strikes.

Kou's eyes couldn't keep up with a single one of them.

With a horrible sound, the kihei lining the walls slid apart. They had been sliced into three. Their corpses fell to the path, Type B, Type A, Special Type, and Full Humanoids all together.

Masses of organic components littered the ground. But Millennium Black Princess didn't show any change.

Despite the slaughter of what appeared to have been her followers, she still stared ahead in boredom.

Sasanoe chuckled again, and Kou could tell he was honestly enjoying himself.

"... Princess!" called Sasanoe, saying his Bride's name for the ... with a graceful nod, still expressionless.

... writhed, then morphed into ... kihei with

... his silver sword ...

Sasanoe stabbed forward and ... bullet.

Millennium Black Princess swiped one wing, stopping the blade, ... casually brushed it away. Sasanoe momentarily stepped back. She was unharmed.

But Sasanoe whispered with pleasure, "You moved."

"...So it seems. A bit, hmm," she murmured languidly.

Kou gaped, amazed that she could speak.

All the while, Crimson Princess was moving. She thrust her slender chest forward, arching her flexible body in a dance-like motion. Her liquid wings detached from her back and changed into a massive whirl-pool of silver. She launched it all forward.

"...Oh?"

The sound Millennium Black Princess made was verging on impressed, but her eyes were still weary, like someone watching a dog performing the same old trick.

The liquid swirled through the air and rushed forward. It bore down on Millennium Black Princess, sweeping up the corpses of kihei as it did.

Everything was swallowed by the brutal vortex. Silver washed away all. Not a single kihei remained.

But Millennium Black Princess stayed as she was.

"Yes, we're done here," she said with a slight tilt of her head. She was still unwounded. She let out a leisurely yawn.

Sasanoe's mouth curled into a grimace. Sounding slightly irritated, he muttered, "Not a scratch on you, huh? She's not hard—or soft; it's just not getting through…"

"…So… Should I? Shall I call him over…? Should I…? Hmm… Boy," said Millennium Black Princess, not listening to Sasanoe. She waved one white hand slowly, gently calling someone over. It wasn't directed at Sasanoe. A lethargic finger raised to point at Kou.

He had no idea what was happening, but she was definitely pointing toward him. He held his breath, not responding. Eventually, she murmured again.

"Come here, boy. Let's have a little chat."

Her voice was filled with a sugary sweet poison.

* * *

"…What? Does that kihei know Kou?" asked Hikami.

"No idea. All I know is we absolutely cannot listen to it!" whispered Mirei.

The two of them pushed Kou farther back.

Kou turned his thoughts to the person he'd met the other night. There she was in his mind, looking so sad.

Was that all real, then?

This whole time, White Princess had remained silent. She just clung tightly to Kou's arm. Her fingers were still shaking slightly. He squeezed her hands tightly in his.

"I'm not going anywhere, White Princess."

"…What's wrong, boy? Come here," said Black Princess, head atilt. Her lustrous black hair shifted and poured over her shoulder. The chains at her neck swayed. Her heavy wings shifted, and she started to move forward. Sasanoe stood in her way, his cloak fluttering.

"Wait. I'm your opponent, correct? Isn't that how it should be?" he said.

"Saying it doesn't make it true. You are no match for me, nor is your little Princess. Give up, okay?" said Black Princess lifelessly. She sounded like she was trying to persuade a child.

Her statement shocked Kou.

The Princess Series surpassed all other kihei, and Sasanoe was a Princess's Groom. Black Princess was stating without a doubt that she outranked Pandemonium's most powerful members.

moment, Kou was staring, wide-eyed.

red.

rd directly into Black

a wing.

fluid sword sha

being forcefully cracked.

Sasanoe gasped and leaped backward,

on him.

His stomach was torn open. Red burst from the wound.

Millennium Black Princess hadn't moved an inch, and it wasn't just that Kou hadn't seen it. She actually hadn't moved, Kou was certain. All she had needed to cut Sasanoe were the air currents created by her feathers as they danced around her.

Sasanoe pressed a hand to his stomach. He was bleeding badly, but it seemed the wound itself wasn't that deep. He leaped back farther.

Black Princess stepped forward and whispered sweetly, "Now, boy."

"I won't let you go," interrupted Sasanoe. He stepped forward and swung his broken sword.

Millennium Black Princess didn't resist. The blade struck her white skin again and again. Even injured, Sasanoe continued the fight, but no matter what direction he tried to cut from, the sword couldn't pierce her.

Without thinking, Kou shouted, "Sasanoe!"

"I know. Shut up, fool," replied Sasanoe, not mincing words. He struck Black Princess's face again. As always, she made no attempt to evade; she just took the hit. Suddenly, Crimson Princess jumped out from behind Sasanoe.

She swung her wings down like a massive ax. It was an attack that could crush a Special Type into dust.

But Black Princess didn't evade that, either. Kou could already tell.

Even an all-out attack by a Princess Series...is nothing to her.

The Princess Series was superior to all other kihei, and the Phantom Rank stood above all others. In short, it was clear that no one in Pandemonium could hurt Millennium Black Princess.

With a hint of pain in his voice, Sasanoe accepted that. "...I can't cut her, so I can't kill her, huh?"

"Yes, very logical. Such a good boy for figuring it out. Try again later, okay?" said Black Princess listlessly. But Crimson Princess hadn't given up yet.

She had kept her silence until now, but it seemed she had a certain pride as a Princess.

With one liquid wing, she forced Sasanoe back. Her other wing rapidly rotated, gaining speed. Then she launched a sharp, slashing attack.

In a low voice, Sasanoe tried to hold her back. "Don't be a fool, Crimson Princess!"

"...How tedious," said Black Princess, a hint of irritation clouding her eyes. She gently waved a hand, her white fingers stroking the air. Hundreds of feathers stirred into action, every one shooting into Crimson Princess's body.

Her whole body shook violently.

One half of Pandemonium's best limply crumpled to the ground.

* * *

Sasanoe didn't hesitate a moment. Leaving himself open, he dashed across to Crimson Princess and gathered her in his arms.

Her body was racked by minute tremors, and she coughed up blood.

White Princess whispered, "She should still be able to initiate self-repair...but if she takes any further attacks..."

Millennium Black Princess tilted her head to the side, then peered at her hand.

For some reason, she was making a face like she wasn't sure what she had done. Eventually, she shook her head, and her eyes gently narrowed. Her glossy red lips curved into a shape resembling a smile.

Dreamily, she called, "Boy, come here. Don't be afraid. Come now, come to me. Let's chat."

Tsubaki put her small body in front of Kou. She touched the barrier that Doll's Guardian had made and peeked out. Hikami and Mirei ~ood side by side. They stepped forward together and made Yaguruma

"Can we at least make sure Kou escapes?"

an open-

her silver

with some beside Kou a...

The bubble-like fluid vibrated, emitting

"*I admit, we have no chance of winning—or none that* likely, *nothing's going to work on her. But we can create a distraction. There's no reason to think we can't. I will do it...so take Kou and White Princess and run.*"

Kou was taken aback. He hadn't expected to hear his name from Sasanoe, too.

In a panic, Kou shouted, "You can't, Sasanoe! Crimson Princess is injured!"

"*Stop with the unimaginative replies. Conversing is a waste of our time. Crimson Princess is injured, but I'm still the strongest one here. You two dying would be a waste, too. The seventh Princess is special; make her your priority. The rest of you act as guards. Live—and make it back to Kagura.*"

He sounded determined. Crimson Princess squeezed his hand. Mirei and Hikami nodded gravely. Tsubaki's and Yaguruma's expressions were more conflicted.

Kou looked at White Princess. She raised her head and looked straight back at him, peering deep into his eyes. She'd finally stopped trembling. She nodded, and a smile bloomed on her face.

"I understand, Kou," she said gently. "Your fate is my fate, and my everything belongs to you. There's no need to be ashamed. Your decision is the correct one." She'd been terrified until a moment ago, but now she swept that fear aside. "I am proud to be able to make this decision with you."

"…Nothing makes me happier than to have you by my side," said Kou with a heavy nod.

White Princess's smile was kind and beautiful. Kou focused on her expression as he made his decision.

"…Thank you, White Princess." He spoke with genuine adoration straight from the heart.

"You don't have to thank me. I fear nothing so long as you are with me."

They expressed their feelings to each other without ever saying exactly what they meant.

Meanwhile, Sasanoe was counting down.

"Three, two…"

Kou squeezed White Princess's hand. She gripped his back. They laced their fingers together like lovers.

"…one."

The two of them immediately dashed, their hands still locked together.

They slipped past Mirei and Hikami, leaving behind their protective shield.

And they leaped, right in front of Millennium Black Princess, queen of the kihei.

* * *

Kou Kaguro thought.

He thought about how much he hated to have someone's death on his shoulders. How much he hated bearing the burden of another's sacrifice.

How much he hated abandoning anyone.

Yes, he knew it.

Blood, bone, flesh, corpses, flames, tears.

Someone looking oh so sad.

And along with those things, he understood, had understood, since long, long ago.

Which is why Kou leaped forward, together with the girl he loved.

These actions had clearly shaken Sasanoe. After a moment of silence, he shouted, "—! Fools!"

"I'm sorry, Sasanoe! When the time comes, please protect White Princess, take Crimson Princess, and retreat! That's where we need you most!" Kou shouted back. He knew Sasanoe would protect White ⟨...⟩ if it meant putting himself in danger.

⟨...⟩ in front of the queen of the kihei. But then

⟨...⟩ked dumb-

For ⟨...⟩

were. There was a col⟨...⟩

when she attacked Crimson Princess ⟨...⟩

Now she was surrounded in an icy hardness.

"Why, boy?" she asked. "Why would you do something like this. Weren't you just told to run? Why would you ignore that? Playing so carelessly with your life… Why would you speak like that?"

She took a smooth step forward, black feathers dragging along behind her. Several drops welled up and fell to her cheeks. Black tears stained her white skin and ran off to the ground.

Millennium Black Princess was crying.

White Princess spread her mechanical wings and hid Kou behind her. In a sharp tone, she said, "Come no closer! Kou belongs to me. If you wish to speak with him, then I ask you to do so from there."

From behind White Princess, Kou could tell.

Millennium Black Princess, queen of the kihei…

She's broken.

When he looked at her tear-streaked face, he felt a headache come on. It was like someone was clawing through his brain. A sad-looking figure appeared in his mind's eye. Fragments of memories stirred up, then faded away.

He felt like he'd forgotten something.

While he struggled with his memories, Black Princess continued to cry. "Nothing changes. It's always this way, always... Oh, but I knew; I understood. At this point, what am I...what am I still hoping for? If so... Then, with these hands..."

She raised a trembling white hand.

And she disappeared.

Something, a storm, passed by White Princess's mechanical wings. A black-and-white mass crashed into Kou, slamming his shoulder.

"—Gah, ah!"

"Kou!" White Princess shrieked.

Mirei and the others shouted in the distance, too, but Kou couldn't hear exactly what they were saying. His bones broke. His veins burst. His arm was close to being torn off; it was a miracle it wasn't.

The force of Black Princess's hand embedded him into the wall. She continued to push him farther, still crying for some reason.

"Die...just die. Yes, that's for the best. Then, once more...once more," she said.

White Princess tried to run to him, but she was blocked by Black Princess's wings. Black Princess cried as she tried to kill Kou. Somehow, her tears reminded him of a child's.

Her attempts to kill Kou didn't inspire fear within him. Instead, he had one overpowering thought.

...*Why?*

He didn't know why she looked so sad. His heart ached more than his broken arm. Blood poured from his body, but he couldn't care less. All Kou could think about...

"Why...do...?" he said.

"It's over...it's over now. Again, this time... H-huh?" she cried.

"Why...do you look so sad?!"

Kou wanted her to stop crying.

That was why he calmly swung up his leg.

White Princess pulled out one of her feathers and launched it through a narrow gap in the barrier of black wings.

Following the command in Kou's eyes, White Princess used the feather to pierce through the sole of his foot. The tip of the feather rose quickly as he kicked up his leg, the location perfect to strike Millennium Black Princess's back. But she wasn't his target. Not even Sasanoe could harm her; what little skill Kou had surely wouldn't be enough.

At the same time, he shouted.

"White Princess, send it now!"

"I know, Kou. All my feathers belong to you!"

White Princess threw another feather toward Kou's raised foot. The tips of the two feathers struck. The magic within them was fire and ice. They reacted.

An explosion burst out behind Millennium Black Princess. Only her

[text obscured by image distortion]

Just as Kou

nium Black Princess. Yet there was something he hadn't

well.

The strength in her arm didn't waver even a fraction.

He wouldn't be able to escape like this.

It's no good…

Kou readied himself for death. But Millennium Black Princess stopped crying. Her tears dried.

Kou was relieved. For some reason, that was enough for him.

So long as you've stopped crying, then I…

"—Break!"

Sasanoe quickly stepped in. He swung his sword, even knowing he couldn't cut her. He struck the silver into her throat.

She completely ignored the attack. But she did release Kou.

She stumbled far back on unsteady feet, shaking her head over and over.

"Ah, aaah… Your coordination is different… I see; you've learned…

So that can change… That's good… With that…with that…," she said with an odd hint of joy in her voice. Her expression was completely different from anything she'd shown so far.

Millennium Black Princess looked like a little girl, practically jumping up and down with joy.

Kou was hit by an intense headache and cradled his head in his hands.

All the while, Sasanoe didn't let up on his attacks. He thrust his sword in toward her chest. White Princess rushed over to get Kou. She picked him up in her arms and began healing his wounds with nanobots. Mirei and the others leaped out from behind the wall.

Millennium Black Princess didn't care about any of this. She kept smiling in delight. Suddenly, she raised her voice in joy.

"With that, just maybe, you can reach me!"

Her wings snapped open.

Black feathers fell like snow.

She rose into the sky…

…and disappeared.

* * *

"Hey, welcome back. Sasanoe already filled me in," said Kagura with a wave when they returned.

Kou stared. Kagura looked particularly shifty today. He sat on top of the lectern, kicking his legs. Eventually, as if it was entirely unimportant, he said, "…So I hear you ran into Millennium Black Princess?"

There was no one else in the classroom currently. Only Kou had been called there.

Each member of the expedition squad had taken their turns getting angry at Kou and reprimanding him, before heading back to their individual rooms. Sasanoe's flurry of insults, in particular, remained on Kou's mind.

"You fool, moronic fool… You fool; you're a fool!"

That's when Kou learned that Sasanoe was the kind of guy who stayed angry and had a very small vocabulary.

Back in the Pandemonium classroom, there were no windows, but the area was filled with the stillness of night.

Kou met Kagura's eyes. In a serious tone, he asked, "What is she?"

"Millennium Black Princess is the queen of the kihei."

Sasanoe had already said as much, but Kou had never heard of the kihei having a queen. She was a strange being. Kou tried to put his doubts and dissatisfaction into words.

But Kagura spoke first. "There's always a king or queen of the kihei. They're a powerful being that all the other kihei obey. They don't usually act, though, since kihei don't usually form groups. The king or queen just exists. They don't give orders, and they don't typically show up near the surface of the ruins. That's why it's rare to have one identi-

_____ in a generation. Most of the time, they're more like something

_____ story, he continued.

_____ ly appeared

Prin_____

secret. In some way_,

issue is that she came out by her own

Kagura pointed at Kou with a grin. Kou squeezed _

By now, his sudden willingness to die had faded. If White Prince _

hadn't been there, he would have met his second death.

Kagura thumped the lectern and continued with a strange rhythm. In an almost a singsong voice, he said, "I saw it coming, but it's still an oddity. Kihei moving in groups, an attack from Millennium Black Princess… So then, putting that together…what happens next?"

What he said sounded ominous.

Something came to Kou's mind, and his expression turned icy. "You can't mean…?"

"Yep, that's exactly what I mean."

Kou thought about that one "exception."

The Academy was surrounded by a high-quality magic wall. While the students did have required military service, there was no risk of a surprise attack from the kihei in the Academy. So one could say it was relatively peaceful.

…Minus that one exception.

"Yep… It's coming. Probably," said Kagura with a strangely calm smile. He closed his eyes for a moment.

Kou turned that prediction over in his mind, the worst possible prediction. It was something he'd worried about time and again since joining Pandemonium.

Kagura put a name to the phenomenon.

"…The Gloaming is coming."

That worst possible prediction tumbled from Kagura's lips.

His voice echoed in the night-filled classroom, then faded.

...she knew the time was

It was unavoidable, and so she could only hope that this time, this time...

* * *

"Kou, does your leg still hurt? You don't look so good," said White Princess.

"No, that's not it. There's just something on my mind," he replied.

He'd returned to his room in Central Headquarters.

White Princess was sitting on the bed with her legs crossed. Kou stood in front of her, mulling over the ominous prediction he'd discussed with Kagura just before. He shook his head and tried to push it away.

I should rest right now. No point in dwelling on it.

He sat next to White Princess, and the thick mattress absorbed the impact.

Silence lingered.

Eventually, White Princess said, "It looks like Crimson Princess will still be able to self-repair. It's thanks to the risk you took. It's good news."

She smiled and looked at Kou adoringly.

He bowed his head in renewed gratitude for this girl who had stood with him in such a dangerous situation.

"Thank you, White Princess…for coming with me back then."

"What are you saying? I belong to you. Staying behind isn't an option," she said proudly, but then her expression suddenly changed. Her face gentle, she whispered, "Actually, that's not quite right…"

She shook her head and pressed a hand to her chest.

Her blue eyes shone, and she said passionately, "Kou, I am truly proud of your decision. Protecting Sasanoe and Crimson Princess was the right thing to do. And it was a kind decision. I love that about you, Kou."

She looked up at him, speaking without hesitation. Another smile grew across her face like a flower opening.

"You are my fate. But the more I come to know you, the more I care for you even beyond that. It's true."

"R-really…? Thank you, White Princess. And you, too—you're more precious to me than anything else."

White Princess was kind to him even though he'd dragged her into danger. She leaned her head forward slightly. He responded by stroking her hair affectionately.

Each word deliberate, he added, "You are my fate, too. I'm not afraid of anything when you're with me."

That was truly how he felt. And it was true when he leaped in front of Millennium Black Princess. If he was holding White Princess's hand, he feared nothing. So long as she was there, he would likely never fear anything ever again.

Yes, even if the Gloaming comes.

Something suddenly caught Kou's attention. He asked again, "White Princess…why were you so scared back then?"

"…That was…"

White Princess had shaken violently when faced with Millennium

Black Princess. That wasn't like her. Kou looked at White Princess with concern in his eyes, wondering if there was some reason for it. But she didn't tell him why.

She just turned her eyes away, thought for a moment, then shook her head.

"I can't...talk about it. I know her...but I don't... I'm sorry. I don't want to talk about it... It's not something I can really put into words."

"Oh...I'm sorry. Don't force yourself if you can't."

Kou reached out a hand. He stroked her head, this time trying to console her. She closed her eyes, seemingly enjoying the touch.

Her entire body was white like the snow. Looking at her ephemeral form, Kou thought.

The unconfirmed seventh member of the Princess Series...and Millen-

...five restarted...

right, should we go to sleep now...

"Yes... And you were injured badly today. You should rest."

Kou nodded at her concerned words, and the two went to lie down, side by side.

He'd already become used to sleeping together. He hugged her, like you might hug a family member. She pressed her head against his chest and gently closed her eyes. It didn't seem like she could fall asleep, though.

She was probably still worried about what happened with Millennium Black Princess. She stirred restlessly.

Kou blinked. He tightened his arm around her back, but she still seemed uneasy. She kept shifting, unable to settle down.

After a little hesitation, Kou started singing.

"The night stars sing for you, the morning breeze waits for you, sweet dreams call to you..."

It was a lullaby that Mirei sung for Tsubaki before, one that Mirei had made up herself. She'd sung in a beautiful voice, Tsubaki's head laid on her knee. Kou clumsily repeated the melody.

He moved his hand along with the lullaby, patting White Princess's back in time with the beat.

Her movements slowed down. The end of the song was coming.

"Good night, sweet child. May blessings find you."

After hearing the end of the song, White Princess seemed to fade into sleep. Her breathing slowed and quieted.

After another brief hesitation, he leaned over and kissed her on the cheek like you might kiss family.

He smiled softly and said, "Good night, White Princess. Sweet dreams."

Beside her, his eyes slid closed, and he whispered a prayer.

Wishing that she would never be alone—and never be sad.

* * *

In the middle of the night, Kou opened his eyes again. He looked around the room. Moonlight poured in through the window.

In that silvery light stood a woman. At first, Kou thought she was White Princess, but she wasn't.

She was wearing a black dress with silver chains sparkling around her white neck. The ends of the chains disappeared into her ample cleavage; she was utterly bewitching. She stared down at Kou where he lay in bed.

Her black hair and eyes were like the night.
Her white skin like the snow.

Kou opened his mouth and called her name.

"… Millennium Black Princess?"

For some reason, Kou didn't question why she was there. Something about this felt oddly familiar. The woman, meanwhile, gazed upon Kou with such lonely eyes.

She opened her mouth, pressed a hand to her chest, and said, "Boy,

I never wanted to hurt you. Or anyone. Not even one... I just wanted to speak with you, to be with you...before the time comes. Just once. That's all I wanted. Please believe me."

She looked sad.

Her warped nature from during the day was completely gone as she desperately pleaded, "...No matter how broken I am, that is all I wanted."

He didn't know why she looked so lonely.

And so he pulled back the covers and reached out his arm. However, his hand didn't touch her. Her body was an illusion. His fingers raked through the air, but she didn't move.

"It's nighttime; you're not going to sleep?" he said, noticing himself ⸺ it was an odd thing to ask. But he was still half asleep, and he ⸺ Black Princess hesitated

Black Princess's eyes widened. ⸺ singing slowly, so that Millennium Black Princess, far away, wherever she was, might sleep. "Good night, sweet child..."

"May blessings find you." Black Princess sang the last line of the lullaby. Kou's eyes opened wide.

"Huh...? That song... Mirei made it up...but you know it?" he asked.

She nodded innocently, then immediately shook her head. Her black hair swished, and Kou caught sight of something blue sparkling.

She smiled forlornly and softly began to fade away.

Her body disappeared into the night.

Only darkness remained.

Eventually, morning came. But there was no one in the room besides Kou and White Princess.

It must have been a dream.

There was no way the queen of the kihei would come visit him.

That was the only explanation Kou could think of.

* * *

"Check." Hikami placed his king in front of Kou.

"Cheater," said Kou without a moment's hesitation.

They were in the courtyard in Central Headquarters. The six of them were spending their time as they liked below a blue sky.

Time had passed since Kou's conversation with Kagura, without event. Months had gone by.

Nowadays, the group of six spent their time together, almost like a family.

Tsubaki would do whatever she wanted, Hikami would chide them, Mirei would smile, and Yaguruma would follow them from behind. And White Princess was always by Kou's side.

That's how they spent every day.

At that moment, Kou was absorbed in a game with Hikami. It was a strategy game that had developed independently within the Academy. The goal was to occupy the most territory on the board.

Considering the size of the pieces, the game was often praised for making it impossible to cheat. But Kou was starting to feel like something was off as he watched the end of the game play out. His eyes suspiciously roved over the soldier pieces scattered across the board, shaped as foxes and cats.

Hikami narrowed his one eye not concealed by bandages. He laughed in amusement and said, "You're right; I'm cheating. You've got good intuition. But just pointing it out isn't enough; you've got to prove where the cheat is. Only if you manage that will I acknowledge your win."

"You know, he said the same thing to me once. It was too much trouble, so I just kicked everything over," said Mirei.

"Guess that puts an end to the issue," muttered Kou, and Mirei smiled gracefully. Kou unconsciously hunched his shoulders. Mirei was always merciless with Hikami. Perhaps remembering the incident, Hikami shook his head.

"My, my, Mirei's a little too violent. Don't you agree?" he asked.

"...I think it's kind of nice," said Yaguruma.

"Yaguruma, wait. It's dangerous to say that," said Kou as he gripped Yaguruma's shoulder tightly. Yaguruma's smooth cheeks were tinged red.

Lately, he'd been taking part in conversations more actively. Overall, that was a good trend, but this was bad.

When Kou chided him, he quickly whispered, as if making an excuse, "Of course, my Bride's the most important to me, you know? ...It's definitely not cheating."

"That's not what I'm talking about."

"Oh my, you may have what it takes. Big Sis loves good little boys, too, you know?" said Mirei with an enchanting giggle.

Princess reacted, perhaps sensing something off but now her

isn't getting involved path."

Kou stopped White Princess and Mirei. They were sitting side by side, pouting. Then he vigorously wiped the whipped cream from White Princess's cheek, who was happy to be the center of Kou's attention once again.

During this little kerfuffle, Tsubaki stayed curled up on Doll's Guardian's shoulder, completely unconcerned with the whole thing. She was focused entirely on basking in a puddle of sun. Nonetheless, she stretched out like a cat and suddenly said, "Look, Sasanoe's walking by."

"Hmm? Oh, you're right. That's unusual," said Kou as he stood and stretched himself tall.

Sasanoe was cutting across the garden, his face concealed by the crow mask like always. Crimson Princess wasn't with him, however. It looked like he was heading toward the classroom. If he had some business, that probably meant Kagura had called for him.

Kou stepped away from the shaded table and made sure Sasanoe could see him as he waved.

"Sasanoe! It's been a while. I know it was a long time ago now, but thank you for what you did back then! Have your injuries healed? Has Crimson Princess recovered? Uh, can you hear me? Sasanoooooooooooooooooooe!"

"Shut up, fool!"

"Oh, you responded."

"Look how fast he's walking," said Tsubaki with admiration.

Kou waved his hand some more. Sasanoe walked away on hurried feet.

Tsubaki stared for a while in the direction Sasanoe had disappeared to, then grinned. "I have a feeling the next time I draw kitty whiskers on his face, I'll get a reaction."

"Stop, Tsubaki," said Kou.

"Quit it, Tsubaki. For the love of all that's good, just stop!" cried Hikami.

She frowned in disappointment.

Kou finally turned back to the game board. His eyes narrowed as he thought back over the course of their play.

This was most likely another way Hikami was training him. Maybe it was a kind of assignment to help him develop his analytical capabilities.

He was about to point out the erratic movement of a certain cat piece when it happened.

A solemn sound filled the air.

Clang-clang, the clock rang.

Ding-dong, the clock rang.

Bong-bong, the clock rang.

Then silence finally returned.

The quiet was so intense it pained their ears.

Even after the reverberations settled, Kou and the others remained frozen in place. It wasn't just them. Every person in the Academy was as still as the dead. They all held their breath, trying to confirm the sound they just heard.

Everyone, not just them, everyone knew what that meant. It was the massive clock in Central Headquarters.

The only time it rang was to warn of that one "exception." Its calculations were worked out by diviners alongside special equipment monitoring the kihei as a whole, all from within Central Headquarters. And it had produced a result.

Hikami was the first to break the silence with a low whisper.

"...The Gloaming is coming in ten days."

That was the thing the Academy feared the most.
A massacre had just been announced.

* * *

... Academy appeared peaceful.

And when ...

Ninety percent of Combat and 60 percent of the entire student population would die.

That was the Gloaming, a disaster that occurred only once every ten or so years.

The Gloaming was when every kihei attacked at once.

Kihei didn't typically act in groups, but during the Gloaming, they all rushed at humans in a coordinated blood frenzy. They left the ruins, moving far beyond their usual range of activity, and attacked the closest location with large numbers of humans.

In other words, the Academy.

Perhaps the single most important reason for establishing the Twilight Academy was to prevent such invasions.

The reason students were generally free to choose which department they entered, and the reason they maintained a certain standard of safety and quality of life, was all for this. This was exactly why the Academy had been peaceful right up to this moment.

"Basically, they let you live a nice day-to-day life so you'll man the walls and die when the time comes."

Those were Kagura's blunt words as he rested his chin in his hands.
Right now, he was sitting atop someone's gravestone.
They were gathered behind the Academy, surrounded by gentle rolling hills. And on those hills were thousands of graves.
A testament to someone's death, standing under a clear blue sky. Several graves were decorated with flowers, but most were neglected. Many didn't even have bones buried below them, or so Kou had heard. Empty graves, with no corpses inside.
Between those gravestones sat all twenty-six of the Pandemonium students, wherever they pleased.
This place was a communal cemetery to remember those who died in the Gloaming.
Kagura used one of the gravestones in place of a chair and continued to speak.
"Our only option for the Gloaming is to hold out until the kihei stop their abnormal behavior. And I have an unfortunate announcement. Since this class doesn't exist, there are no public records on it. However, the class that has the most casualties is always our Pandemonium. If we didn't exist, the regular student death rate would surpass eighty percent. We fight until we are destroyed so we can keep their death rate down to sixty."
Kagura was telling them the hard truth.
The students nodded slightly. No one brought up any particular arguments or voiced any discontent. Even Kou accepted it as a matter of course.
Pandemonium had always been the class sent out to the worst battles. Kou had an idea of what would happen the moment the bell rang to announce the Gloaming. Even if someone didn't agree, no one could survive on the outside, beyond the Academy's walls. Even if they cried and screamed, there was nowhere they could run to.

Someone had to stand and fight against fate. It was the same for the other students.

And Pandemonium had their pride.

We are the proud members of Pandemonium.

Our Brides and our skills are everything.

Then, we can't be afraid, thought Kou. As a member of Pandemonium, he, too, stiffened his expression.

That's when one of the other students suddenly raised her hand.

~~lled~~ on her, letting her speak.

~~through~~ the last Gloaming, didn't you?" she

Wouldn't that

Gloaming, Kou

explanation Kou would nev

"I've told you a million times alrea~~dy~~

fighting. If I do too much, it'll shift the world out

pens, the damage won't end with just a little Gloaming. It n

flying in the sky and the land turning to water."

Absurd words came so smoothly from his mouth.

Kou's eyes widened as he wondered what Kagura meant, but the student who had asked just nodded as if she already knew all about it.

It seemed that Kagura's situation was common knowledge within Pandemonium. Perhaps students who had been in the class for a long time had even seen the beginnings of what he meant.

Kou pondered Kagura's power. As he did, he found himself struck by a basic question.

Hikami was sitting diagonally in front of Kou. Kou tapped his shoulder.

"Hey, Hikami. Where's…Kagura's Bride? I've never seen her before…but I assumed he was one of the two teachers married to a Princess Series."

"No, actually, that's two other teachers… Guess you haven't met them yet. Even though they're teachers, they're both assigned to guard the imperial capital. It's hard to tell if they'll be able to return for the Gloaming... Kagura doesn't have a Bride."

"...Come again?" Kou was taken aback.

Kagura was the most powerful teacher. How could he not have a Bride?

"Heeey, don't sit there gossiping in front of everyone; we're in a crisis here," said Kagura. "I mean, actually, it's fine. I'm glad you're feeling so relaxed. But you really should ask me directly. I'm sitting right here, after all!"

He fluttered the hem of his coat playfully. There were shouts of "Stop it!" and "That's so not cute!" The jeers were dutifully consistent.

Kou set about organizing his confused thoughts. Even Sasanoe continuously relied on the power of his Bride's blade. It was hard to imagine someone fighting the kihei alone.

Despite his hesitation, Kou asked, "So you don't have a Bride?"

"Nope. Guess you didn't know, Kou. My alias is Widow... I lost my Bride. Well, more accurately, I consumed her," he replied nonchalantly.

Kou was at a loss for words. He was having too hard a time understanding what Kagura said.

Completely ignoring Kou's reaction, Kagura added, "Actually, two. I consumed two Brides."

Kou was plunged even further into confusion. Kagura kept saying he *consumed* them, but Kou found the word completely unfathomable.

Kagura waved a hand, then held a finger in front of his face and whispered like he was telling a secret, "This is confidential information, too, though I'll let you know... married couples can increase their power by consuming each other. But usually it just ends with the Bride going on a rampage or the Groom dying, unable to adapt. So you shouldn't do it if you care about your partner...though, I did it. All your upperclassmen who have tried have failed. Anyway, be careful, because it usually ends in certain death... All righty, that's all."

Kagura cut off the conversation there. It hadn't helped Kou's confusion at all. He looked at White Princess beside him.

I'd never even considered consuming my Bride.

He desperately held back the bile rising in his throat, but at the same time, he thought back to an earlier occurrence.

White Princess's power had grown when she consumed Kou's blood. He might well have come upon the thought of feeding himself to his Bride, even without Kagura's explanation. But the opposite option was a completely different story.

To Kou, that idea sounded far too horrifying. But Kagura's talk hadn't caused any sort of uproar among the students. This, too, seemed to be common knowledge for the members of Pandemonium. Their shock, repulsion, and revulsion must have run its course long ago. They'd come to terms with all of it, and now they were here.

Kagura clapped his hands together as if to clear the air, then turned

We lie in

us at the end of the night.

without fear. That, my students, is where our pride lies.

Voices of agreement called out one after another. Standing in front of those thousands of graves, not one of the students was afraid.

Kagura tapped the face of the gravestone he was sitting on with his heel. He gazed at each of his students' faces and said, "Should any of you think this is pointless, you are welcome to give up the name Pandemonium and flee. I won't chase after you."

"You've got to be joking."

"Cut the crap."

"Don't treat us like we're little kids."

"We are Pandemonium."

"Our Brides and our skills are everything."

None of the students wavered in their responses. Their voices were filled with an unyielding strength.

Kou looked around at everyone.

Hikami narrowed his one eye. Mirei smiled. Tsubaki yawned. Yaguruma stared forward, looking stern. Sasanoe's face was hidden. But there was no sign of fear in any of them.

There was a variety of replies, but all their answers were the same.

Kou reached out a hand, and White Princess reached back with a smile. They twined their fingers together tightly.

They felt the same as the rest of Pandemonium. There was nothing to be afraid of, so long as they were together.

Kagura nodded at his students' response. He let out a boisterous laugh and said, "Good, it's decided! Everyone kills or is killed together! So long as strength remains in us!"

"Of course."

"What else would you expect?"

"It's our honor."

"That's who we are."

Proud voices called out.

And Kou realized that while the Academy was plunged into despair, here at least, there was hope.

But that wasn't because they believed in survival.

Their human pride shone brightly, stronger even than the despair of death.

* * *

"...Kou, can I have a moment of your time?"

After the special lesson in the graveyard, White Princess hesitantly voiced her invitation.

Everyone in Pandemonium had returned to the classroom.

With the Gloaming predicted to happen in ten days, the regular students were likely submerged in panic and misery, but that uproar didn't extend to Central Headquarters.

The classroom was pleasantly bubbling with excitement.

Every member of Pandemonium was throwing themselves into training. Many of them were aiming to improve their coordination with their Brides by the time of the Gloaming.

The bulk of the squad's strength came from the Brides. The Grooms couldn't afford to hold them back. That's why it was essential for them to improve their synchronization. Flower Rank, Wasp Rank, and Demon Rank were practicing with special fervor. Every once in a while, someone would get blasted into the air.

Some others had spread out documents from past expeditions and started a meeting to discuss strategy. Sasanoe was among those.

Normal classes had been canceled, and that meant they were free to go as they pleased.

White Princess looked unhappy as she looked up at Kou. He bent ____ so his eyes were in line with hers. He raised a hand and ____ hair. A heartfelt smile spread across his face, ____ course. My time is always meant to be ____

____ somewhere I'd

Kou ____

From the side, ____

and Grooms to treasure ____

curfew during an emergency, but ____

Don't forget! Ah!"

"Hikami! I can't tell if you sound like a mother or a father, and focus on your own training! You'll die right away if you don't improve your battle skills, too! And you're being ridiculous anyway!" retorted Mirei. She and My Kitty were running Hikami and Unknown down.

Hikami barely managed to block Mirei's roundhouse kick, while Mirei winked toward Kou and White Princess as if to say "Have fun."

Beside them, Tsubaki was nodding. Hiding behind the shield of Doll's Guardian, she muttered, "I see you two are progressing. I can tell. You'll get bit if you get in the way of love."

"…Go on, get out of here. But it gets cold at night, so wear something warm if you're going to be out late," said Yaguruma as he eyed Tsubaki for an opening.

Fire Horse couldn't go all out while indoors. So instead, he was adjusting her firepower and looking for a fighting style with increased efficiency. As he was fighting, he suddenly raised his hand to stop Tsubaki and said, "Wait a second, Tsubaki. Agh!"

"Oh, oops. I can't stop all of a sudden. That was my fault," she said as Yaguruma sat on the ground, having taken a wall to the face. It was a direct hit.

Kou rushed over to Yaguruma and knelt beside him. "Yaguruma, are you okay?"

"I-I'm fine. More importantly…" He raised his head despite pain causing his body to shake.

It looked like Tsubaki was holding back as well. Yaguruma didn't even have a nosebleed or broken teeth. Kou was relieved.

Yaguruma rummaged through his inside pocket before pulling something out and saying, "This is for you."

"What is it…?" asked Kou as he looked at the objects.

It was a pair of beautiful earrings. They each had a blue magic-imbued gemstone set within delicate silverwork, their overall shape like a flower.

Kou looked between Yaguruma and the earrings, wondering why Yaguruma would give him such a gift.

Yaguruma gave a quick nod and pointed at the earrings. "They look like plain jewelry, but they're not. It's a prehistoric communications device. I got them from an Exploration student I saved when they were in a tight spot. One person puts blood inside, and another wears the earrings. Then the two can communicate at any time."

"They seem really valuable; why would you give them to me?"

"My Bride is Fire Horse. We're not using them, so I'm offering them to you. It's handy for you to be able to communicate during battle… And I bet *she'd* be happy if you gave them to her."

Yaguruma kept his voice low and cast his gaze toward White Princess, then quickly turned back to look at Kou. He suddenly clasped his arms around Kou's shoulders, took in a breath, and let it out.

With a vigor appropriate for a classmate of the same year, Yaguruma said, "Good luck on your date!"

"Thanks! I'll do my best!" Kou instinctively matched Yaguruma's energy. The pair exchanged a firm handshake.

In that moment, Kou and Yaguruma forged a strange sense of unity. Kou thanked him again and went back over to White Princess.

Hikami, Mirei, Tsubaki, and Yaguruma watched the two of them.

Kou and White Princess raised their joined hands high. "Thank you, everyone!" Kou said. "We'll be back soon."

"Yes, sorry to leave you for now!" White Princess called before she rushed off with Kou. They left the hyped up classroom behind.

And that was when they entered the ruins.

longer hoped to ~~~

She waited, alone, for the day to come. She trembled, ~~~ ~ ~ ~
memories for support.

Her memories of that short time she was able to meet him.

That, held within her heart, was all that kept her going.

Just a little longer.

Just a little longer.

And surely everything would change.

* * *

"Why here?" asked Kou immediately after they arrived. He looked around, visibly confused.

It was easy to slip out of the Academy with the amount of chaos the prediction of the Gloaming had caused. There was a large group of students at the gates, but Kou and White Princess simply flew over on

White Princess's wings. Once they were on the outside, it was easy to get into the ruins.

Their exit went off without a hitch, but that wasn't the problem.

Kou never expected they would be heading to the ruins.

And this particular location held very specific memories. He and White Princess first met in the upper levels of the ruins.

When Kou asked why they'd come here, White Princess pressed a hand to her chest. She timidly replied, "Kou, I told you before... I feel as if a part of me is missing. We must do something to survive the Gloaming. I don't want the people I've become close with to die. I need all of my functionality now...which is why I'd like to take back what I am missing."

"Oh...uh, so... This is because you can't do a complete adjustment of your wings in the Academy?"

"That is another reason," she replied with a shake of her head to indicate that there was something else. She then explained her primary goal. "I want to confirm what it is I'm lacking, and I'd like to go to the place we met in order to do that."

"That 'birdcage'?"

Kou thought back. He was reminded of the intense pain from when he fell through the hole in the reinforced glass and slashed open his stomach, but he shook his head and pushed that aside. The fact was: This is what White Princess wanted. He should make it happen.

"Okay, White Princess. Let's go... But I only know one way there, and I can't guarantee it'll be safe. By which I mean... Um, it's pretty dangerous. But as long as you're okay with that."

"I don't mind, and please don't worry. No matter which path we take, I will protect you."

White Princess squeezed her hands into fists. Kou stroked her head affectionately. He knew how she felt. He was weak, but he still planned to protect her no matter what happened.

They looked at each other, smiled bashfully, then nodded.

"All right, let's go," said Kou.

"Yes."

They ran off, hand in hand.

Kou's squad from the Department of Magic Research had been

attacked here before, but this place had originally been a Clean Zone. The two made quick progress without meeting any significant danger.

Kou remembered the path to the deep hole. While he was running, he had barely been aware of his actions, but he would also not easily forget his brush with death and the unending fear he had experienced.

The problem was that they would need to fall down the hole.

* * *

"White Princess, grab my shoulders there… Yeah, uh-huh. That should be okay…"

"Are you ready, Kou? I think it's time we fell."

…uld be able to hold on to him in

unknown black metal and …

ical devices embedded in thick vegetation, but Kou lacked the kno…

edge to determine what they were. At the center was a strange glass case, still intact, that resembled a casket.

There was no one inside the case now.

Tattered cables littered the area, and a mysterious solution flowed out of them, only noticeable on close inspection.

Kou and White Princess landed nearby with a thud. She pointed to the empty case and said, "I was in there, right?"

"Yeah… Huh? Don't you remember?"

"I think I had memories of it long ago, but they were wiped away by the shock of our fateful meeting and all the happy memories that followed. My name is White Princess; my alias is Curtain Call. That is all I have from then… But, Kou. Kagura has called my alias ominous many times. I hadn't thought about it until now."

What did "Curtain Call" mean?

As White Princess whispered, Kou had his own questions.

A curtain call is when the actors come onstage to greet the audience after the curtain has fallen at the end of the play.

Why was that her alias?

Why was the seventh Princess made? A Princess who doesn't exist…

Those answers might be here.

White Princess approached the glass case and wiped away the dust gathered on top.

Her brow furrowed, then she walked up to an apparatus near the case. After a moment of hesitation, she wrote prehistoric characters on the panels. It was like her finger moved on its own, following some subconscious memory. She rotated the panels, realigned them, and entered a key in accordance with some unknown rule.

"This is the release key for information concerning me, I think… If there are any records about me still here, this should bring them up…," she said.

Other characters appeared above the glass case. Tiny notes rushed across the display.

White Princess stopped moving. Her eyes flicked back and forth rapidly.

Kou stood beside her, but he couldn't read the primitive writing. White Princess seemed able to, though. Her wide eyes were fixed in place, like large blue gemstones.

Whatever was written there, White Princess started to tremble.

At first, Kou was hesitant to ask about it, but he made up his mind and said, "White Princess…what does it say?"

"Kou, telling you this would… No, I can't hide this from you. That would be unforgivable."

She shook her head and stepped softly back from the glass case.

Her mechanical wings burst open. The surrounding vegetation was slashed and torn. Millions of petals fluttered about. White flowers, nearly silver, flitted through the air.

They momentarily froze before plummeting to the ground.

The wings spread out into the surrounding area. There was a flash of blue light and a harsh, grating sound of machinery operating. The wicked metal parts glittered.

She slowly blinked, then looked toward Kou.

Again, the thought struck Kou.

Her blue eyes were like the sky, her white hair like the snow.

She stretched out her hand. Kou moved his arm in response. They linked hands, like always.

White Princess closed her eyes, then opened them. She folded her wings and said, "Kou, listen to what I have to say. If you wish to end our marriage after this, please say so. You have that right. You have the right to run from me, to forget my love."

"What are you talking about?"

"Curtain Call is a weapon built for extermination." White Princess's voice suddenly grew cold.

Kou blinked. He didn't understand what he was hearing. The only thing in front of him was a beautiful girl. Nothing about her matched. But White Princess was serious.

White Princess and the other members of the Princess Series.

It was a story from long, long, oh so long ago.

The world was at war and had been for a very long time, and the countries were exhausted. Weapons development had reached its final stage. One country in particular, renowned for its magic technology, set to work creating the Princess Series. And once they had finished, they used what they had learned to achieve their ultimate creation.

It was the result of broken minds and the flawed convictions they were driven to, the creation of a group of magic weapons developers amid a rampant apocalyptic ideology.

It would truly "bring an end to the war." It was the final weapon, a weapon that would destroy the world, including its developers' own country.

When everything was over, there would only be this single being, bowing on the stage in the sky.

Curtain Call, the exterminator.

But she didn't wake.

Without her activation, the end of the world slumbered for a long, long time.

And that was a blessing for all.

A joyous, wonderful blessing.

Or it should have been.

"Of course, I am lacking," said White Princess. "I am incomplete… But even though I am unable to wield my full power, for some reason, I awoke when I swallowed your blood… I should never have been activated. And it's not too late. You can still end our marriage."

"White Princess."

"Even I cannot estimate my true power. I can't be sure I wouldn't harm you—"

"White Princess!" shouted Kou, forcing her to stop talking.

Silence filled their spacious surroundings.

Despite her words, she looked on the verge of tears.

He felt like he'd seen her innocent look, forever ago. Again, he thought, *I don't want her to cry. I don't want her to isolate herself.*

There was no one except White Princess who filled the hole in his heart. He patted her head, the head of the end of the world, as if nothing was wrong. Trying to persuade her, he said, "You are already my everything."

She looked up in surprise. He stared into her blue eyes as the words followed naturally.

"I love you, White Princess."

It was a direct, certain confession of unvarnished truth.

White Princess blinked. She tried to say something, but Kou took her hand and continued.

"From the very beginning, you've felt as if I was your fate. I can't say the same for me… At first, I was just overwhelmed. But as we've spent time together, I've come to love you."

"Kou, you…"

"I love your childlike expressions. I love when you smile beside me.

I love your silky white hair and your slender, soft fingers. I even love your mechanical wings. Whether you're hanging out with everyone or protecting me, I can't help but think how happy that makes me, how cool you are, and how much I love you... I love you far more than you could ever think I do," he said with a smile.

Those were his true feelings; that much he was sure of. It was hard to believe he was the same person who had had such dulled emotions in the past. Now he felt so much warmth from her being beside him. He adored her.

She was someone he could call his own.

His precious Bride.

And more than anything, she was a wonderful girl.

[text obscured] I don't care what you are. Even if you are the end of the

[text obscured]

survive. Along

He took her hand and squeezed it. Then he took *[text obscured]* ruma gave him from his pocket. He bit his finger and put a drop of blood in the center of each of the blue gemstones.

Lifting up White Princess's hair, he put them on her ears.

They dangled behind her hair, both communications devices and beautiful jewelry.

"With these, you can talk to me at any time. We'll always be together," he said.

He pressed his lips to her fingers, returning the gesture from some time before.

White flowers, nearly silver, rustled around them. Amid this hallowed scene, he made an earnest vow.

"I give you my trust, my adoration, my fate. This I swear, White Princess: I will protect you for your sake."

*   *   *

White Princess leaped from the ground. The flower petals cut earlier jumped into the air. She embraced him, laying her cheek against his.

Like a parent cuddling a child, like a lover caressing their beloved.

And she returned the vow, even more determined than ever before.

"I shall be by your side for all eternity. I give you my restraints, my servitude, my trust... This I swear, Kou: I shall kill any death that comes for you."

The two embraced ever so tightly.

And with that, they made a promise.

A promise that couldn't be broken.

Just like a real bride and groom.

Because they loved each other so earnestly.

The Bride of Demise

This time.
This time.
Let it go well this time.

No matter what awaited at the end of it all.

* * *

Ten days later, the fated time arrived.
   A sea of disaster and hell.

The Gloaming.
This was the beginning of an all-out attack by the kihei.

Standing atop the magic wall that surrounded the Academy, Kagura made a declaration.

"Pandemonium's goal is simple. Don't bother with the little ones. You're going to crush whatever is coming from the ruins' lower levels."

Kou nodded, the high-altitude breeze striking him. The path on top of the wall was steel gray, and it boasted a panoramic view.

He was wearing a fox mask, a vermilion cloak fluttering about him. The Pandemonium students were wearing their formal uniforms, each one matching. They looked like a group of inhuman creatures defending the Academy.

Only Kagura looked like his usual self as his voice rang out.

"Information on the queen has been passed to all students. We don't know what causes the Gloaming. Maybe if we kill her, something will change. But even Pandemonium will be fighting a defensive battle against the queen. Your goal is to slow her down as much as possible. I pray that you don't die too soon."

It was a coldhearted speech, but Kou nodded slightly. This conclusion was already obvious based on Sasanoe's battle with the queen. Not even Crimson Princess's attacks could scratch her. They currently had no potential strategies for taking out Millennium Black Princess.

There was likely no one in the Academy who could harm her.

Kagura's footsteps rang out as he walked across the top of the wall.

"Our goal is to defend the Academy until we die. Kill until you are killed. Go as long as you still have life."

His order rang out. All twenty-six of them nodded. Silence fell, but it didn't last long.

Clang-clang, the clock rang.

Ding-dong, the clock rang.

Bong-bong, the clock rang.

The grand sound was their signal.

In the distance, the horizon turned black, as if night was bubbling up from the earth.

Strange forms like insects, like beasts, like machines, stained the world.

The kihei horde came.

As they appeared, Kou and the others could feel vibration beneath their feet. Machines chimed and groaned like a kind of music.

The magic wall had woken.

Massive contraptions moved. Mechanical wings and legs unfurled at a steady rhythm. Similar to how a flower changes shape when it blooms, the magic wall transformed. The wings and legs cast sharp outlines against the sky.

As the wall moved, a spark burst out from it like a shooting star.

The next moment, there was an explosion in the distance, and kihei were sent flying. The horizon melted red. But new kihei came forward, reclaiming it. The magic wall fired its second shot, exploding more kihei.

The loud noise continued.

The mechanical wings and legs chanted a song of destruction.

Kagura stood unfazed amid the shock waves whipping toward them, glaring at the ground.

"This should keep most of them at bay…but others will be here any

there. They were

pered, "…Burst."

He snapped his fingers once, and hundreds of kihei exploded.

Kou gasped. The attack was beyond logic; it surpassed immutable laws.

Kagura lowered his arm. The contour of his cheek seemed to phase out for a moment. He bitterly muttered, "That's about my limit. I'll work with the wall and do what I can to hold back any kihei that make it to the Academy. The rest of you, cut through the enemy lines and destroy the kihei that came from the ruins' depths."

He raised an arm again, and the black feathers scattered. They fell through the air, like snow.

The darkness danced at his will as he murmured, "…Move out."

One after another, the students leaped from the wall. Their cloaks fluttered as they fell from on high.

Using the power of their Brides, they landed on the ground far below them. Those with lower athletic ability were helped by other students.

Alighting on the battlefield, the members of Pandemonium freely left the Academy behind.

Masks on their faces, they hurried toward nearly certain death.

Before White Princess and he leaped, Kou looked at Kagura.

Kagura faced his students, childlike words on his lips that seemed to take every ounce of his strength to say.

"Good luck."

Kou leaped from the wall, Kagura's words drifting behind him.

With White Princess by his side, he cast himself into hell.

* * *

In the blink of an eye, the members of Pandemonium had moved beyond the firing range of the magic wall.

The Phantom Ranks stood at the head of the twenty-six-person squad.

Besides Kou and White Princess and Sasanoe and Crimson Princess, there was a black-haired girl named Yurie with her Full Humanoid Bride and a well-built boy named Shirai with his Special Type Bride, making a set of four pairs.

They cut down the hordes of weak kihei. But as they'd expected, most were aiming for the people gathered at the Academy, not the combatants right in front of them. The Phantom Ranks decided to overlook most of the kihei that ignored them. The magic wall and Kagura would be enough to destroy those.

Pandemonium had a different target.

That which must not be allowed to reach the Academy. They must kill it or hold it back.

Kou and the others cut down anything they came in contact with in that hell, pinned on every side by grotesque forms.

If they were simply students from the Department of Combat, there wouldn't be a single one of them left standing by now. Pandemonium, however, continued straight ahead through the waves of kihei. Eventually, the black horde faded. They'd quickly cut through the first enemy line.

Empty space continued for some time.

Then Pandemonium came upon the second enemy line, their target. They were at a point halfway between the known ruins and the Academy.

There was a massive horde of kihei, all Type A, Special Type, and Full Humanoids that came from the depths of the ruins. Their numbers were already above one hundred. Adding in those kihei that joined later, there were likely more than a thousand.

That was when it hit Kou. There were twenty-six members of Pandemonium, including the fragile Flower Rank.

And this won't be a quick fight.

On that grim battleground, Shirai made the first move.

"Now, my Bride. Nameless, make the earth tremble. Sing your love

add its

Pandemonium.

As they did, Doll's Guardian and the other defen... their move. They built walls at calculated locations, forming a protective bulwark. These walls would block the enemy, preventing them from overrunning the group all at once.

"Preparations complete? Nice. Not bad," said Sasanoe, standing at the front of the trench. He drew his fluid sword. Silver spread in waves, glinting in the sun, then instantaneously snapped together and returned to its sheath. The heads of twenty kihei rolled.

Yurie nodded lethargically. She rubbed her eyes, yawned, and said, "My precious Sister... I leave their punishment to you."

The Full Humanoid Bride named Sister moved. Her appearance was that of a beautiful black-haired girl who looked similar to Yurie. Sister launched out countless steel wires, and thirty kihei were suspended in midair.

Kou entered the trench as well. White Princess released flashes of blue light to protect him.

"Let's go, Kou. I am always with you," she said.

"Yes, let's, White Princess. And I am always with you."

He hadn't given her his blood this time. White Princess was a weapon of extermination, and they had to consider Kagura's warning. This would be a long battle, and they needed to avoid strategies that could result in White Princess going berserk.

Besides, when she had drunk his blood, she had emitted a strange black light. It was like an all-consuming darkness. He didn't think that was something they could control. It was best not to use a weapon you couldn't handle.

Everyone was moving now. Those who specialized in midrange attacks fired at the kihei from inside the trench or from behind walls.

The main battle was just getting started.

Many of the kihei were destroyed by the Brides of the Phantom Rank members. Crimson Princess's silver buckshot and White Princess's blue light mowed them down with precision. Nameless swallowed many whole. Sister mercilessly flung her steel wires. Sasanoe, too, ran across the battlefield.

Any kihei that somehow made it past them were slaughtered by the Demon Rank students. My Kitty weaved through friendly fire, and Doll's Guardian threw walls in all directions.

The Wasp and Flower Ranks were in support roles. The medic squad maneuvered deftly as the more powerful students protected them.

The Brides were the major players in the battle. Their Grooms were primarily providing rear support and giving commands.

In the trench, Yaguruma pulled his scarf away from his mouth and whispered, "Onward, Fire Horse... You run beautifully."

His Bride raced off, setting ablaze a dense group of kihei.

The battle was going in Pandemonium's favor. But Kou could tell. This was what had happened last time, too. He analyzed the battlefield through White Princess's eyes.

There's a limit to how many kihei each Bride can take down.

More kihei were coming, a horde of hundreds expanding in front of them.

Sasanoe must have decided this was a good time, because he started giving orders.

"Yurie, Kou, take out any that get close. Shirai, expand our defenses. Get rid of the other walls for a minute."

Yurie brushed back her hair and nodded timidly. Shirai continued slaughtering kihei without saying a word.

The Phantom Rank members created an opening for the other Brides to retreat. Tsubaki and the others took down the walls. Sasanoe checked that all preparations were complete and nodded. Then Crimson Princess spread her arms.

Sasanoe's order rang out. "…Clear them out."

Crimson Princess's body bent gracefully. Her wings detached, and she created a whirlpool of silver. It shot forward, washing away all kihei in its path. It seemed she couldn't use her bigger attack repeatedly, _____ it once, she went back to firing off scattershot.

Amid the battle,

"Yeah, it won't be too long now," replied _____ wolf mask.

Eventually, Kou's predictions proved true. Several of the weaker Brides were showing more severe signs of exhaustion. More and more kihei were getting through the line. A number of ominous shadows appeared in front of the trench.

Kou removed his mask and held up both hands as he called to his beloved.

"White Princess!"

"Kou, may the fortune of war smile on you. Call me if you ever find yourself in danger," she replied, launching two of her feathers in his direction.

He grabbed them and leaped from the trench, blades in hand.

Then he split the Special Type kihei before him in two.

* * *

Organic components from kihei littered the ground, human blood and organs mixed in among them.

Kou didn't know whose they were, but their twenty-six members were beginning to dwindle.

Broken masks fell to the ground. Screams echoed, then ceased.

They slashed and sliced their foes, but the onslaught never ended. The strength of the Phantom Ranks was the main reason they were still standing.

Sasanoe continued to fight cleverly, Yurie beautifully, and Shirai powerfully.

The other students were only fighting the kihei that escaped the Phantom Rank's attack range, but each and every one of those kihei had enough power to breach the magic wall if they were to reach it. Originally, they would have been beyond the capabilities of humans.

Kou gritted his teeth and lopped the head off a Full Humanoid in front of him.

Ever since the incident in the ruins, his coordination with his Bride had increased even further. He was able to pull off techniques no average person was capable of as he let White Princess's swords guide him. He didn't even hesitate when facing an enemy with a human appearance.

There was nothing but death here.

Live or die. Kill or be killed.

Faced with those choices, there was no room for doubt.

The hell continued.

Other than Kou, none of the Phantom Rank Brides or Grooms was showing any signs of fatigue. So long as things continued this way, they might be able to keep fighting until the battlefield was cleared. The problem was everyone else.

Barely managing to swing his own blades, Kou checked how his friends were doing.

He was relieved to see them all standing. Though, narrowing his eyes, he could see things weren't ideal. Each of them was wounded, Hikami looking particularly worn down.

He was a Wasp Rank, after all, meant for support. He wasn't suited for direct combat.

"Hikami, fall back!" Mirei shouted. "More and more kihei from the deeper ruins are joining. You and Unknown will have a hard time. Stay behind!"

"Hmph, I used to be in Combat. Besides, I can't provide information in these conditions unless I'm up front," said Hikami bitterly as he threw aside his broken mask. His Unknown was currently split into eight pieces.

Hikami was their eyes in this chaotic battlefield. The medic squad, in particular, was getting valuable information from him.

But suddenly, his face froze. Whatever he saw, it caused him to yell, "Mirei, watch out!"

"Hikami?"

He shoved Mirei aside, and that's when Kou saw it, too.

Destruction.

The next moment: *bonggggggggggggg*.

Instruments blared, out of place.

Petals fell.

Pink and red and black and white and gold and silver.

Magnificently.

Gracefully.

Gloriously, the colors fell.

Bong, bong, the bells rang.

Between the chimes came the *huff, huff* of breathing.

A flag swayed high in the air. It was red, with some meaningless scribble resembling a crest. Below the flag were marching kihei. Beast shaped, frog shaped, fish shaped, insect shaped, human shaped, all different kinds marching at their own pace. Each lifted a leg in their own way and turned.

All the kihei raised their voices at once.

"Her Highness is arriving, Her Highness is arriving, Her Highness is arriiiiiiiiiiiiiiiiiiiiiiving!"

The metallic declaration rent the air.

A curtain of darkness fell. The chains binding the wings came undone midway and faded. Then the pitch-black wings snapped open.

A beautiful woman of black and white appeared.

Millennium Black Princess.

Queen of the kihei.

* * *

"Hikami, who told you to take my place?! Are you trying to burden me with regret for the rest of my life?!"

"…S-sorry. I just decided on my own. Don't regret."

"I don't care what you say—I'm going to! Yes, you can't stop me!"

Mirei was shouting as she dragged him into the trench. Kou, Tsubaki, and Yaguruma followed. Mirei cast healing magic on him, but the wound was deep. The bleeding didn't look like it was going to stop.

"…I'll keep the kihei away. You stop the bleeding," said Yaguruma.

"Leave defense to me. No one will get past me," said Tsubaki.

Yaguruma's Bride trampled the kihei near the trench to death, and Tsubaki formed new walls.

Kou raised his head. White Princess and Crimson Princess were facing off against Millennium Black Princess. None of them were moving, but Kou could tell that if White Princess left, Crimson Princess would be killed.

It wasn't a good time to ask her to heal Hikami with nanobots.

Kou racked his brain, trying to come up with a solution.

While the rest of them were frozen with anxiety, Hikami moved. He pressed down on his wound as he stood.

Blood cascaded to the ground. Tsubaki shouted, "Why are you moving, you moron?! Do you want to die right now? Idiotic moron!"

"I don't, but…with Millennium Black Princess here, we're all going to end up dead if we don't do something. Right? Then I might as well give it a try. And if White Princess is freed up, she can heal me," he said with unbelievable composure. Then he did something no one expected.

As if it were perfectly normal, he started to undo the bandages covering his eye. No one dared ask what he was doing, wounded as he was.

There was a sort of reverence in his motions.

Finally, they saw something emerge from beneath the cloth. They were at a loss for words.

In Hikami's left eye socket was a smooth white spherical object.

It was an egg.

Dumbstruck, Mirei said, "Hikami...you... Wait, that can't be!"

"Yeah, it's Unknown's egg. It acts as a lens that operates in place of my eye. Most people think I can't see with this eye, but truth be told, I can see through the gaps in the bandages. That's how I cheated, when people let down their guard... And then, the eye that I lost..."

_____ ddly shaped eye. Where had the original eye

was as low as possi___

Bride die with me unable to do anything.

"Hikami... You've lost your mind," muttered Mirei in a strained voice. Kou was thinking the same thing.

No one in their right mind would give someone their eye "just in case."

"I agree with her," said Yaguruma.

"Hikami, you've gone way past moron and into something else," said Tsubaki.

Everyone's voices were strained and their expressions stiff.

But Hikami still smiled gently as he continued.

"Ha-ha, I realized something when my Combat squad was all but annihilated. Death's smile is capricious. No one knows when it'll turn their way. And I'm saying no thanks to watching my Bride and my friends die."

His expression suddenly turned sour. It was a ghastly look Kou had never seen him make. What sort of things had Hikami seen in the past?

"If I have to experience a hell like that again... My eye is a small price to pay," Hikami whispered. "I have to try everything I can."

And now was the time to use it.

Lowering his voice even further, he looked directly at Kou and said, "...You mind? From this point on, I'm taking a gamble on my beloved wife and you Phantom Ranks."

Kou nodded. No one had ever been able to kill the queen of the kihei in the past, nor had anyone found the means to do so. But now, just maybe, there was a chance of them shaking that immovable wall.

Because what Hikami was doing was so abnormal.

It might just be enough to knock fate off course.

* * *

This raised a question.

If every Bride ate each of their Grooms just before the Groom died, would they have a chance at victory?

The answer was no. The Brides would go on a rampage, resulting in even more casualties. This gamble was only possible because Unknown wasn't originally specialized in battle, and Hikami had made a series of adjustments beforehand.

It wasn't easy to gouge out your own eye, modify it, and have your Bride eat it in advance.

But Hikami had done it.

And it drastically changed their situation.

Using a small Flower Rank kihei, the plan was conveyed to all Phantom Rank members. Kou contacted White Princess directly using the communications device and was surprised when an illusion of himself appeared beside her. This device didn't transmit just voice, it also sent an image of the speaker. Millennium Black Princess didn't react, meaning he was able to convey every detail of the plan to White Princess without issue.

Hikami had Unknown recombine her eight pieces.

Mirei sat beside him, her arms crossed. She let out a slight sigh and said, "We don't know how this will turn out."

"Nope... If it goes south, run. This is my choice," said Hikami.

"Don't be an idiot. We're in it together until the end. Do you really think I would leave you alone at this point? No matter what happens to me or my Bride, we're staying. Friends are precious… You're the one who says that all the time, right?"

"Ha-ha… So I'm a super-considerate guy who loves his friends?"

"No one said that…but yes."

Their usual exchange was just a little different this time.

That's when Millennium Black Princess made a move.

"…Are we done yet? Would you all just die?" she said.

Her wings snapped open, breaking the silence.

The momentary gentleness she possessed last time was gone. The Kibei rampage had apparently taken hold of her as well. She had an _____ _____ presence befitting a queen.

_____ _____ _____ light flashed in

The first volley was _____ diately launched hundreds of black arrows at _____ Crimson Princess. They used their own wings to brush aside the fragments coming in from all directions.

Then the two closed in on Millennium Black Princess and attacked. Silver fluid wings and mechanical wings swung down. Black Princess didn't block, but no attack damaged her.

"You know it's pointless…," said Black Princess.

But the two kept attacking, their fruitless attempts repeated over and over.

From behind them, Unknown hid herself and approached. She twined herself around Millennium Black Princess.

"…Hmph, you worm."

If she wanted to, Millennium Black Princess could kill Unknown instantly, but she didn't resist. Perhaps because Unknown couldn't harm her. She just shook her head languidly.

It was the arrogance that came with absolute strength.

Hikami snapped his fingers. "The time has come. My wife, consume me!"

Something dissolved inside Unknown. She let out a wordless roar and changed dramatically before their eyes.

Unknown's power cracked through the bounds of the ordinary, reaching something previously utterly impossible.

She bared her sharp fangs and snapped her jaw closed on Millennium Black Princess. And her fangs pierced the skin.

For the first time ever, tiny holes opened in Millennium Black Princess's body.

But that was all.

"…Pathetic."

This time, Black Princess went to shred Unknown, but White Princess struck down with her mechanical wing. Even so, the slash had no effect. The mechanical wing stopped at Black Princess's throat.

But while White Princess attacked, Unknown was able to make her escape.

That same moment, White Princess made a huge jump and detached her own wings. Bringing them together, she transformed her wings into a massive sword.

She turned the tip of that sword toward Black Princess. As she thrust the blade forward, she shouted, "It's up to you, Crimson Princess!"

"…Understood."

For the first time, Crimson Princess responded with words.

Her body bent, and she detached her wings again, launching off a vortex of silver. It crashed into the part of White Princess's wings that served as the hilt of her sword, forcing it forward like a mallet striking a chisel.

The two plunged the blade into the hole from Unknown's bite.

The wound tore open, but White Princess's wings shattered into a million black fragments.

Just then, Shirai and Yurie whispered their commands.

"Now, huh? My beloved Nameless, overflow."

"Sister… There's a bad little girl over there. Rip her apart."

The first voice was forceful, the second listless.

Nameless poured himself into Millennium Black Princess's wounds, then Sister's steel wires focused on that area and tore it apart. The wounds worsened, but Black Princess launched the two kihei back.

"How dare you touch me," she said, sweeping her black wings as if in annoyance.

Sweeping them farther back than she needed to.

Kou and Sasanoe immediately rushed in toward her exposed torso. Each of them held in their hands a feather taken from White Princess's wings in advance.

The magic within them was fire and ice.

They drove those two feathers toward the wounds in Millennium Black Princess.

l·l"

The attack·

With just a little more, the tips of the blades would touch, and Black Princess would die. Hikami's ingenious plan had finally destroyed the wall no one had ever surpassed.

Kou kept pressing on the sword, not relaxing a fraction. Black blood spilled out; flesh tore.

...*Just a little more!*

Then Kou raised his head.

And he saw it. Her.

Millennium Black Princess.

* * *

Her arms hung limply. She didn't resist, despite being a step from death.

Kou held his breath. A question appeared in his mind.

Was she really rampaging like the other kihei?

All she was doing was looking up at Kou. She opened her mouth slightly, then closed it. An innocent smile appeared on her lips for the first time.

As if to say she was so utterly relieved.

As if to say this was how it should happen.

Like she'd found a place to go home to.

Again, Kou thought.

Her black hair and eyes were like the night. Her white skin like the snow.

Without her snarling expression, she looked just like *her*.

A portion of her black hair was suddenly cut, revealing her ear. There hung an earring of delicate silverwork. In the center…

…was a beautiful, shining blue gemstone.

It was a communications device in the form of an earring.

When he saw that, Kou's eyes opened wide.

It was the exact same as the ones he'd given to *her*.

Kou thought back to the visions he'd been having, the ones he thought were dreams.

Why was an illusion of Millennium Black Princess appearing before him?

Why did she know the song that Mirei made up?

Why did Kou feel such nostalgia whenever he saw her?

I finally understand.

Someone looking so incredibly sad. Someone crying.

Someone's childlike gestures replayed in the back of his mind.

He'd finally realized it. The reason he got a headache every time he saw Millennium Black Princess, the reason he felt like his memories were all mushy and mixed together.

The reason he didn't want her to cry.

Kou finally realized who that "someone" was who had been in his memory this whole time.

She's… White Princess. But she's also not White Princess.

Pulling back with all his strength, he stopped his blade.

That single moment was a betrayal of everything, but he couldn't help it. His eyes filled with tears, and his chest burned. As if in response to his overwhelming emotions, he stopped attacking.

Sasanoe noticed the change. Deciding it was impossible to carry out on his own, he instantly retreated.

Only Kou remained.

He stood in front of Millennium Black Princess.

And he asked her.

Why was she crying?

Why did she know Kou?

Why did she have the communications device?

the lullaby?

And just

The Bride of Demise

Several Grooms had their Brides consumed... extend the Brides' lives. In the end, both partners died. Only White Princess lived. It was a result of Kou giving her a portion of his flesh and blood before he died.

She didn't go berserk. She was the only one who managed to adapt.

She didn't know why.

She was just left there, all alone.

A curtain of silence and darkness draped around her, only herself and countless corpses inside.

Hikami, Mirei, Tsubaki, Yaguruma, Sasanoe.

And Kou Kaguro. They were all dead.

No tears flowed from her eyes. Mere crying could never express the depth of her emotion.

She thought back to a scene of blooming white flowers, nearly silver.

To that exquisite, wistful backdrop and the promise they made.

Finally, she whispered.

*   *   *

"Though you may become broken, beaten, or lost, I shall be by your side for all eternity."

And so White Princess consumed what remained of Kou's corpse.

The blood smelled of iron, the flesh reeked, and the bones were hard.

It was nothing more than an object, but once she had consumed it all, she began to change. She didn't know why, but Kou Kaguro's combination of flesh and blood was special.

In that instant, Curtain Call was complete.

She was the broken dream that people saw on their deathbed.

She was meant to use the magic formulas contained within her wings to reverse the flow of time, to exterminate each country *before* the wars had begun. That was the reason she had been created. Her wings had been granted the power she would need to rescue the world from the very root of war. By consuming Kou Kaguro, she had activated those magic formulas.

Now she was using that for a different goal, her goal.

The light that flashed from her wings was not her usual blue but a black. It enveloped her wings completely, and she leaped into the air.

Then she disappeared from the world.

That moment was the start of her experiment.

She had made a promise to him.

A promise that couldn't be broken.

"I shall be by your side for all eternity. I give you my restraints, my servitude, my trust… This I swear, Kou: I shall kill any death that comes for you."

Before, that promise was a blessing. But now it had become a curse.

To save Kou Kaguro, White Princess activated her abilities.

In the beginning, she thought it would be simple.

All she had to do was make sure Kou Kaguro survived the Gloaming. But he continued to die.

She went back in time, but Pandemonium was destroyed even though she assisted them.

She forced Kou to escape Pandemonium, but then he was among the 60 percent of regular students who died. She made him flee the Academy and tried protecting him herself, but he was caught and executed as a deserter.

She killed every person who might be the cause of Kou's death, before they could kill him.

Then Kou killed himself.

She chose not to bind herself to Kou, but in the end, he still died in the Gloaming. After repeating the events over and over, she finally went back and tried to protect his parents, to prevent Kou from ever entering the Academy.

But she realized that, for a certain reason, that was impossible.

kihei themselves. She tried to return

she made a cruel and perverse

She would go back in time over and over again and consume
and sometimes herself.

Through this, her power grew.

Each time she did so, her hair and eyes turned blacker. Her wings changed, and her body developed. Even as she lost herself, even as she was worn thin, she killed the current king of the kihei. But his magic was immediately passed on to a successor.

During the Gloaming, she took down the king and saved Pandemonium. But it shifted the world out of phase.

After trying time and time again, White Princess finally learned.

The world wouldn't allow significant interventions by those who weren't meant to be there. Kou Kaguro himself would have to change fate.

She went back in time, to before the Gloaming. She waited until she was naturally chosen as the queen. She abandoned the name White Princess and called herself Millennium Black Princess instead.

*   *   *

After fifteen thousand tries, she found herself here.

And this time, she had confirmed something.

Kou was White Princess's Groom. And he also had an ever-so-faint connection to Millennium Black Princess, the first White Princess. That was why he experienced so much déjà vu, why he was troubled by faint memories of "someone familiar," why his coordination with White Princess was improved. The Kou Kaguro of this time should be able to kill the queen himself and survive the Gloaming.

That's why Millennium Black Princess chose to let herself be defeated. What would happen after he killed the queen with his own hands was, as of yet, unknown territory.

She didn't know what would happen. But the moment she'd waited for would surely come. It had to.

From the bottom of a crucible of searing, dreadful magic, she begged.

This time.

This time.

Let it go well this time.

Even if at the end of it all, her own death awaited.

But now Kou had seen it.

* * *

Kou quietly looked at Millennium Black Princess.

The only likeness that remained was her skin, white like snow. But because they were connected, he could tell. There was no doubt that she was also White Princess. She was none other than the person he cared for most, at the end of a brutal transformation.

The current White Princess simply looked distressed. With a glance, Kou urged her to go heal Hikami. He turned back to Black Princess.

Speaking gently, he said, "You're White Princess... I don't know how you became the queen of the kihei, but I know you're White Princess. Let's go home; don't fight us here like this."

"Boy...no, Kou... I can't, I can't..."

Black Princess took an unsteady step back. A jet-black tear, mixed with altered magic, ran down her cheek.

She cried, covering her face. Shaking her head, she pleaded, "You weren't supposed to notice. I have to be Millennium Black Princess. I have to be killed here. That's why I…I had to shoot at Mirei, so Hikami would protect her as I predicted, and it would act as the trigger… I have to be struck down. If I'm not, fate won't change… I…"

Her hands gripped her shoulders, the nails digging into her flesh, blood running from her white skin.

She trembled. Holding something back, she desperately continued her words.

"   The Gloaming happens when the king or queen of the kihei gath-

_____ berserk. I took over the role of queen

_____ have a

"I'll kill you and she

A massive amount of magic shot through her body. wings enlarged. Their jutting branches filled the air like a cosmic tree. Despair itself grew at a terrifying rate.

Every single thing was consumed, then eroded.

It was all penetrated by jet-black darkness the color of ink.

* * *

Black.

Something black fell.

Like snow.

Like rain.

Like ash.

It swallowed everything in sight.

In the beginning, the black was shaped like feathers, but the plumes disappeared without a sound. The blackness lost its complexity, forming a simple sphere. From there, the change continued. The sphere became a flat plane, then expanded again as a cube.

Then it burst.

Millions of needles, pointed at every living thing.

Hikami covered Mirei, but they were pierced through the back together.

A mist of blood dyed the air.

Doll's Guardian gathered Tsubaki in his arms, but he was shattered. Her small body was held aloft by the needles, her doll-like form filled with countless holes and transformed into a grotesque corpse.

Yaguruma rushed toward Fire Horse, but his legs were skewered. One needle caught on a portion of intestines, dragging it up and out as it traveled through his mouth.

Sasanoe immediately flung Crimson Princess away. But the moment he died, she stopped resisting. Instead, she chose to cradle his corpse in her arms. Two of their most powerful were gone.

It all happened faster than the blink of an eye.

But the needles didn't touch Kou.

A moment before they did, Kou was nearly smothered in mechanical wings. It didn't hurt; the wicked-looking metal didn't actually touch him. They were just covering Kou, like they were hiding something precious.

Relieved, White Princess whispered, "Good. I made it in time."

She hadn't protected herself.

The black silently tore through her.

She coughed lightly. Blood dribbled from her lips.

Kou didn't fully understand what had happened. He reached out his trembling hands and hugged White Princess. Almost beside himself, he slipped his arms past the mechanical wings, wrapping them around her slender, fragile body.

"White Princess, White Princess, White Princess!"

"…K-Kou…"

The thorns slipped out of her.

Losing her support, she managed to regain her footing, just barely. The light was already fading from her blue eyes. She could most likely no longer see. But she still protected him desperately.

"Kou," she whispered. "I have a request…"

"What is it?"

"I want you…to consume me…"

Kou's eyes opened wide. He tried to move his mouth, to ask what she was talking about.

Even then, blood was still pouring in rivulets from her mouth. Despite those streams of red, she pleaded with him.

"I knew… Black Princess was me, after consuming you… That's why I knew her…when we first met… I was afraid of the truth…so I couldn't say anything…to you…"

A single tear fell to her cheek. Her voice was filled with pity and sorrow.

"She…I…must have tried so many times…but it still wasn't

[text obscured] you to c-consume me… Grooms can con-

[text obscured]

a gentle voice, she [obscured]

"For me, for Black Princess who tried to p[obscured] times… For you—and me…please…"

"White Princess…"

"Kou…"

Suddenly, her heels lifted.

And she gently brought her lips to his.

The taste of blood and a slight warmth spread over his lips.

It was the end of their first and final kiss.

White Princess smiled. In the most tender of voices, she said, "This is my curse on you, Kou… Somehow…live…please…"

Her eyelids closed. The strength drained from her body, and she collapsed in Kou's arms. Her mechanical wings wavered slightly, but they stood fixed in their protective shape around Kou.

Sound disappeared from the world.

The White Princess in his arms now looked just as she did when she was sleeping.

But something was clearly different.

...I can't hear you.

There was no sound of her breathing or of the operating of her organic components.

White Princess—I can't hear you.

Kou Kaguro understood.

This was death.

He would walk that same path soon, most likely. Driven mad with grief as he was, he wanted to make that choice. But he couldn't. He was cursed.

With their first and final kiss, he had been left a request. He couldn't betray that.

That is why he hugged her corpse to him and whispered:

"Once again, I vow. I give you my trust, my adoration, my fate. This I swear, White Princess: I will protect you for your sake."

And so Kou sank his teeth into White Princess's windpipe.

At this point, the Groom would usually die. But unluckily, Kou Kaguro was an exception. He had learned about White Princess's abilities. He had also understood what she suspected about Black Princess.

In that moment, Kou Kaguro began a hell that seemed like eternity.

And now every one of the twenty-six members of Pandemonium was dead.

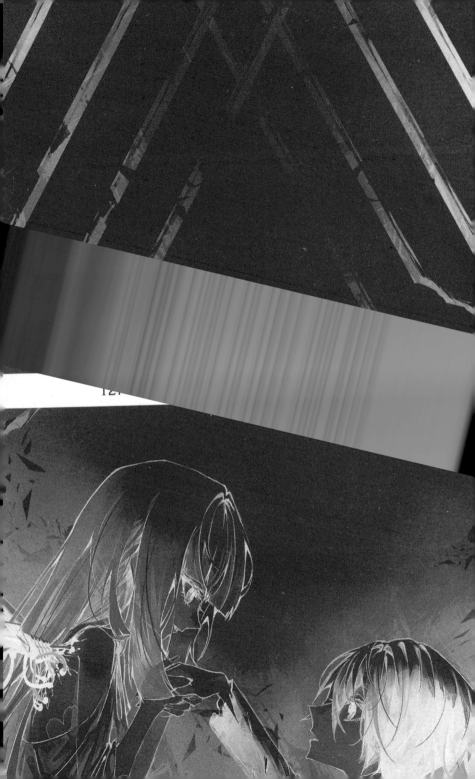

It was a ...

"Kou, are you awake?"

Kou Kaguro opened his violet eyes.

Someone's face entered his blurred vision.

Just then, a single tear ran down his cheek.

"...Huh, that's weird."

With a tilt of his head, he reached a hand up to his eye. Kou didn't usually cry. In fact, he couldn't remember ever crying, no matter how sad something was. But now he couldn't stop.

He was baffled by the tears that flowed without reason. Before him, a girl with vaguely childlike features similarly tilted her head in confusion.

"Hmm? Kou, are you crying? Why?"

"I'm not sure... Maybe I had a bad dream?"

"I don't think I've ever seen you cry. I wonder what you were dreaming about," she said, mystified. Her large chestnut-colored eyes complemented her short brown hair.

Kou took in her full form. She wore a vermilion uniform and hugged a textbook and several research books to her chest.

He recalled what he knew about her.

She was Asagiri Yuuki, a girl in the same year as him.

He blinked several times. He felt like he hadn't seen her in long time, but he didn't know why he would feel that way.

He cocked his head and asked, "Asagiri, was I…sleeping?"

Asagiri's eyes widened, then a gentle smile spread across her face.

"You're still pretty out of it, aren't you, Kou? You just said yourself you probably had a bad dream. And can't you tell if you were sleeping?"

"I don't know if that's necessarily true. Right now, I can't tell… Actually, you're right, I'm definitely spacing."

He turned his from head side to side. He felt like the remains of the strange dream were still stuck to his eyeballs.

He rubbed his eyes, then looked around. He was in a large room. The windows on all four walls were hidden behind closed black curtains. On top of the scarlet carpet were rows of chairs facing the center of the room.

He was in a massive, tiered circular lecture hall.

Kou suddenly dropped his gaze. There was a messy scrawl written in his notebook.

"History can be divided into two major periods:
"Before the kihei appeared and after."

"You just get fed up hearing about it so much, don't you? I know I'm sick of it," said Asagiri with a sigh.

"Yeah, I can't say it's interesting to hear about something you already memorized over and over again…so…"

Kou's jaw dropped. His memories had finally caught up to him. Everything he had experienced, everything he would experience after this, came flooding into his mind.

He realized he'd sent himself back. The moment before Pandemonium was wiped out, he had used White Princess's ability to go back in time.

Yes—he understood. He traced his own messy handwriting with his finger and forcefully whispered, "So then… *That's enough of here.*"

Kou Kaguro's vision twisted and swirled.

Everything went black, as if a curtain dropped before his eyes.

His surroundings began to shift.

The change happened so quickly, like someone flipping through the pages of a book they were bored of rereading.

* * *

White Princess used her mechanical wings to send everything—even her body—back in time. Kou, however, wasn't capable of such a feat.

All he could do was move his consciousness to various points along ʰᵉ timeline.

close his eyes, and his consciousness would be ᵗⁱᵐᵉ and place. Apparently, he was ᵉˢˢ's magic formulas. If

Kou Kag

Asagiri's call echoed deep

His vision was filled with green.

This was just before they would be attacked by the kihei.

In front of him was a "window" made from very pure magic crystal.

Some sort of ivy-like plant swayed on the other side. He couldn't feel the flow of air, though, wearing full magic armor as he was. He was having difficulty breathing and tried to rub his eyes, then realized his hands couldn't directly touch his face through the armor. He gave up and shook his head.

"No, this isn't the place… Definitely not," he said.

"Kou, what's wrong? Kou?"

"All right, another try."

Kou Kaguro's vision twisted and swirled.

Everything went black, as if a curtain dropped before his eyes.

* * *

Kou Kaguro opened his violet eyes.

Crimson blood streamed into them. His vision was hazy and red.

He narrowed his eyes, checking whether he'd made it to the place he was aiming for.

He did notice a beautiful "something" in front of him.

In a space that resembled a birdcage, there stood a pure-white thing.

Her blue eyes were like the sky, her white hair like the snow.

In a daze, Kou thought about what was in front of him.

…Ah, finally, once again…

The beautiful girl stretched out her hand. Kou instinctively moved his arm in response. Intense pain shot through his entire body, but he forced his hand up. Even so, she was too far.

…To you, I…

She blinked. She ripped out the cables connected to her body and walked forward. When she reached Kou, she took his hand. Something extended from her back.

The surrounding vegetation was slashed and torn. Millions of petals fluttered about. White flowers, nearly silver, flitted through the air.

They momentarily froze before plummeting to the ground.

Amid this hallowed scene, the girl took a knee.

She pressed her lips to Kou's fingers.

"From this moment on, you are my master. My wings belong to you. I am delighted to meet you, my beloved. And oh, how I have waited for you. My name is White Princess. My alias is Curtain Call."

Just like a knight of legend, like a princess in a fairy tale, the awoken girl made an oath.

"Though you may become broken, beaten, or lost, I shall be by your side for all eternity."

Kou remembered seeing this before, in some distant dream.

Along with the shadow of a sometimes childish face and a sad face. Indeed, he remembered it.

Faint tears welled in his eyes.

Blue light fell from her wings, regenerating his wounded body. In the midst of that warmth, Kou whispered, "I've been waiting for this moment forever, too."

"Yes, then we are fortunate. This must be what they call fate."

*   *   *

White Princess smiled.

And so Kou Kaguro began again.
He began the fight to take back the girl in front of him.

* * *

Kou's goal was clear and simple.

He would ensure White Princess and Black Princess lived—and that Pandemonium survived the Gloaming.

In order to do that, he needed to suppress Black Princess's rampaging magic. But there was a problem; he wouldn't be able to manage that if _____ right now. He needed to repeat his life

battle, there were some _____

One of those was his body.

When White Princess traveled back, she could add strength to her body in addition to her mind. Yet even after countless attempts, she still couldn't save them from the Gloaming. And Kou could do even less.

No matter how much Kou struggled, he was unable to break through that last barrier, the final battle.

It seemed utterly impossible to keep both Millennium Black Princess and White Princess alive in the same attempt.

There might very well be a future for him if he abandoned Millennium Black Princess. But that would mean forsaking the life and the emotions of the original White Princess. She may have been changed irrevocably, but Kou couldn't bring himself to kill her, not after she had tried so hard to protect him.

Kou was prepared to continue his own experiment for as long as he possibly could.

And so he dug himself ever deeper into his hell.

*   *   *

"Come on, now, is that all? That's not even enough to rival a Demon Rank!"

Tsubaki was chattering in her high-pitched voice. She waved her finger in a little dance.

This was the first thing that had happened after he'd been welcomed into Pandemonium.

Walls flew at Kou again, this time from the left and right. He ducked his head to evade them so they slammed into one another. Then he flipped out from underneath and kicked the new wall that had appeared in the air above. And using the counterforce from his kick, he pierced the wall behind him with his sword.

Each time he made a move, jeers and cheers bubbled up in the classroom.

Kou continued to slice through the combinations.

In reality, he wasn't even looking at the walls anymore. He'd already memorized how each attack came—and from which direction.

The walls were appearing more quickly and moving faster now. But it didn't matter.

He kicked off a wall coming from above and rotated. With legs spread and body flat, he cut apart a wall below him. Pulling the sword back up, he rolled to the right and pierced the wall on the left. His mind was blank as he moved.

He went as fast as he could go, slicing through wall after wall.

"Ah, good! It's not cute, it's not lovely, but it's not bad either! Now let's get serious! I, Tsubaki Kagerou, will crush you, here and now!"

Walls immediately appeared around Kou in every direction, forming a caved-in sphere with Kou at the center.

The next moment, the walls closed in on each other.

With Kou in the middle.

It was the same as always. The important thing was searching for every possible option between now and the Gloaming. This point in time didn't actually matter.

He heard Hikami's voice and whispered, "White Princess… Give me another feather."

"Understood, Kou. I give you my control, my support. Everything I am is yours."

White Princess had immediately released a feather from her wing. It pierced into the sphere from the outside. Kou pushed his own sword into the wall from the inside. It was a tandem attack from both sides.

The magic within the feathers was fire and ice, and the violent reaction between the two exploded the sphere. The walls shattered into ˺ flew in every direction.

˹rd of rubble just before it began to fall.

ˉˊˎ force, zipping through the

"—:

"…Ah…"

He was too fast. Kagura's hand didn't

A red line spread around Tsubaki's neck, then split op˹

Crimson blood gushed out, soaking the classroom. Tsubaki's cherub-like face was frozen, her jade eyes open but unmoving.

Her body collapsed to the ground, nothing to hold it up.

Doll's Guardian groaned in despair. He reached a trembling hand out to Tsubaki.

Kou looked at his own blood-soaked fingers. Tsubaki was sprawled on the ground in front of him, like some inanimate object.

She would never flash her teasing smile again.

It was his fault.

As screams burst up around him, Kou shook his head.

He squeezed his eyes closed.

He would try again.

* * *

A black-and-white mass crashed into Kou, slamming his shoulder.

Millennium Black Princess's face was right in front of him.

For a moment, he was confused as to where he was.

"—Gah, ah!"

"Kou!" White Princess shrieked.

Mirei and the others shouted in the distance, too, but Kou couldn't hear exactly what they were saying. His bones broke. His veins burst. His arm was close to being torn off; it was a miracle it wasn't.

The force of Black Princess's hand embedded him into the wall. She continued to push him farther, still crying for some reason.

"Die…just die. Yes, that's for the best. Then, once more…once more," she said.

White Princess tried to run to him, but she was blocked by Black Princess's wings. Black Princess cried as she tried to kill Kou. Somehow, her tears reminded him of a child's.

Her attempts to kill Kou didn't inspire fear within him. Instead, with adoration in his voice, he shouted, "You're White Princess, aren't you?"

When he did, her eyes opened wide. She trembled slightly.

In as gentle a voice as he could manage, trying not to upset her, he said, "It's fine… It's all right. You don't have to protect me anymore. Quit being the queen of the kihei; just run. If you do…then I can finally give up."

"No! No! I can't!"

"It's okay, it's okay…White Princess."

"No, no, no, I caaaaaaaaaaaaaaaaaaaaaaaan't!"

Millennium Black Princess snapped.

Her fingers dug into his shoulders; more and more blood poured from his wounds. She reached a hand to his neck, and there was no life in her eyes anymore.

It seemed that all that remained in her deranged mind was the thought of starting over again.

Kou's neck snapped.

* * *

With mere seconds to spare, Kou Kaguro opened his violet eyes.

"Kou, are you awake?"

Someone's face entered his blurred vision. In front of him, the still young girl looked at him. Her large chestnut-colored eyes complemented her short brown hair.

Kou could see her entire body. She wore a vermilion uniform and hugged a textbook and several research books to her chest.

He recalled what he knew about her.

Then he said:

"Come on, this isn't the one I need."

* * *

he'd used

wings enlarged.

Every single thing was consumed,

Black.

Something black fell.

Like snow, like rain, like ash.

It swallowed everything in sight.

In that black, White Princess kissed Kou.

Tears streamed down his face as he thought, *One more time...*

One more time.

One more time.

This time.

As many times as it took.

And so...

Every one of the twenty-six members of Pandemonium was dead.

* * *

Three thick slabs of synthetic pâté. Onions, raspberry sauce, and pickles placed between two slices of bread. Then, a knife inserted through the center to keep it all in place, finishing off the huge, glorious tower. Last but not least were the fries arranged around it for decoration.

It did look delicious, but Kou was already so tired of eating it that it might as well have been made from mud.

Kou looked around. Mirei and Tsubaki weren't there. He'd failed to befriend them this time. He hadn't become friends with anyone in Pandemonium.

Nonetheless, Hikami sat with him, looking concerned.

"…Um, Hikami, what is this about?"

"You always seem like you're worrying about something… Honestly, I wanted to ask what was up. Not that I think it's my place to say anything. Anyway, you might as well eat properly. Besides, I borrowed the kitchen to make all this, so just sit back, relax, and eat."

"Yeah, I know. That's just the kind of person you are."

"…You think? Well then, how about you eat?" urged Hikami.

Kou shook his head. They sat in silence.

The trees swayed quietly. Then, suddenly, Kou asked a question. "Hikami…what happened before? When you were in the Department of Combat?"

"H-huh? I don't remember telling you I used to be in Combat…"

"Sorry, I just heard a rumor…" Kou was lying. "I heard that Unknown saved you right before you were about to be killed."

Hikami's right eye narrowed. He gently touched his strange left eye, concealed behind his eye patch. Up until now, Hikami had avoided the topic or remained vague. This time, though, something about Kou must have changed his mind. Quietly, he began to speak.

"It was hell. We ran into an especially strong Special Type… I watched my friends and underclassmen who looked up to me get cut down before my eyes. One after another. Worst of all, it…played… with them while they were still alive. I saw people I was close to lose their ears, their faces split in two. I listened to them beg for death… and all I could do was hold up two of them who were still alive, one on each arm, convince them not to give up, and run."

Hikami clenched his fists, his knuckles turning white. Hatred and rage filled his eyes as he reached the conclusion of his tragedy.

"Unknown was in the direction we ran. It was thanks to her accepting me as her Groom that we survived, just the three of us... I can't even bear to meet the other two, now."

"But..."

"No, I couldn't... I would do absolutely anything to go back to that horrible day... But I can't. You can't bring back the dead. Once it all slips from your fingers...it's gone." He looked at Kou in silence. After a moment of uncertainty, he continued, "...Your eyes look like mine did, ¹ ᵗʰᵉⁿ. That's why I'm worried about you."

"...ᵒ back, you would... I feel the same."

"...ʳʸ much

coming from ᵐᵉ, ᵘ

Kou shook his head again. These ᵤ

Kou knew that. He had a feeling he'd already let many ₚ slip through his fingers. Even so, Kou said, "Thank you, Hikami. ı can't, but I appreciate your feelings."

And Kou closed his eyes.

He did it to return to the time he should return to.

And to cut off Hikami's voice.

* * *

"Good luck."

It was the start of the Gloaming.

Kou leaped from the wall, Kagura's words drifting behind him.

With White Princess by his side, he cast himself into hell.

In the blink of an eye, the members of Pandemonium had moved beyond the firing range of the magic wall.

The Phantom Ranks stood at the head of the twenty-six-person squad. They cut down the hordes of weak kihei. But as they'd expected, most were aiming for the people gathered at the Academy, not the combatants right in front of them. The Phantom Ranks decided to overlook most of the kihei that ignored them. The magic wall and Kagura would be enough to destroy those.

Pandemonium had a different target.

That which must not be allowed to reach the Academy. They must kill it or hold it back.

And Kou had another goal beyond that.

He had already finished picking through all the top-secret documents he could get his hands on at the Academy. He'd been executed several times for that. But even with the information he had gained, he hadn't worked out a way to stop Millennium Black Princess. Despite everything, he had chosen to gamble on the smallest of chances. And so he rushed onward.

Together with the others, he raced through this hell, pinned in on every side by grotesque forms, and punched through the first enemy line.

Then Pandemonium came upon the second enemy line, their target. They were at a point halfway between the known ruins and the Academy.

There was a massive horde of kihei, all Type A, Special Type, and Full Humanoids that came from the depths of the ruins. Their numbers were already above one hundred. Adding in those kihei that joined later, there were likely more than a thousand.

That was when it hit Kou. He could easily cut them all down.

He already knew how each of them would move, where they would come from. But he couldn't get past Millennium Black Princess. He still didn't know how to stop her magic from rampaging. It was his one roadblock.

He slipped through the battle, worrying the entire time. How could he get past this point with both Black Princess and White Princess alive?

That's when Sasanoe called to him with a ghastly look on his face.

"Hey, what the hell are you…? I thought this was your first Gloaming? What are—?"

"I'm sorry, Sasanoe," Kou said gently.

Sasanoe's stomach was torn open.

He had fallen victim to a surprise attack from behind by a Special Type kihei.

Sasanoe's organs fell to the ground with a sickening splat. Crimson Princess screamed and rushed over to him. Her outstretched hand was covered in blood.

It was the twenty-sixth time this had happened. Kou sounded tired of it all as he said, "If you stand there, your stomach will… Oh, I'm too late."

He raised his head, freezing in place.

⸻ looking at him

"I love you, White Princess."

When he came to, he was there. Those words had just fallen from his mouth.

It was a direct, certain confession of unvarnished truth.

White Princess blinked. She tried to say something, but Kou took her hand and continued.

"From the very beginning, you've felt as if I was your fate. I can't say the same for me… At first, I was just overwhelmed. But at some point, I loved you. And now, I do love you… I should love you… I should…"

"Kou, you…"

"I love your childlike expressions. I love when you smile beside me. I love your silky white hair and your slender, soft fingers. I even love your mechanical wings. Whether you're hanging out with everyone or protecting me, I can't help but think how happy that makes me, how cool you are, and how much I love you... I've loved you far more than you could ever think I did. I loved you," he said, crying.

Those were his true feelings; that much he was sure of.

He was bound by that. Bound, forever and ever.

She had been someone he could call his own.

His precious Bride.

And more than anything, she was a wonderful girl.

The person he had to save.

"That's why I need you to tell me, White Princess. What should I do? It's the same, no matter how many times I try again. I can't see a way out. I love you, White Princess; that's the one thing I don't want to lose. But I feel like it's all fading away. Tell me, White Princess, tell me—how do I do it?"

How do I save you?!

Kou screamed, his head in his hands. White Princess was taken aback. All he wanted was for her to hate him; he begged for it, vehemently praying that White Princess and he would be separated.

But she didn't go. She crouched down, her arms hesitantly reaching for him.

She wrapped those arms around him.

Like a mother bird would her chick.

Like a lover would their lover.

Like a wife would her husband.

And she whispered gently, "I don't know what's troubling you, but this I swear."

White Princess gripped his hand tight. She pressed her lips to his fingers, returning the gesture from some time before.

White flowers, nearly silver, rustled around them. Amid this hallowed scene, she made an earnest vow.

"I shall be by your side for all eternity. I give you my restraints, my servitude, my trust... This I swear, Kou: I shall kill any death that comes for you."

*   *   *

Kou laughed. He cried and laughed. No matter how many times he did it over, it was the same. White Princess existed solely for him. That truth was far too painful, too cruel, too saddening, too joyous.

The two embraced ever so tightly.

And with that, they made a promise.

A promise that couldn't be broken.

Just like a real bride and groom.

Because they loved each other so earnestly.

* * *

White Princess smiled. In the most tender ⌄⌄ ⌄ ⌄
my curse on you, Kou… Somehow…live…please…"

Her eyelids closed. The strength drained from her body.

Sound disappeared from the world.

There was no sound of her breathing or of the operating of her organic components.

Kou Kaguro understood.

This was death.

And it was a curse.

With their first and final kiss, he had been left a request. He couldn't betray that.

And that's how he had ended up here.

He hugged her corpse to his chest like a small child, his voice choked with tears as he murmured:

"…Hey, isn't this…enough…? White Princess…can you forgive me…?"

* * *

And so ended the 14,999th trial.

Kou decided to give up.
That he'd had enough.

Kou Kaguro closed his eyes and opened them again.

He realized he was in a pure-white room.

The Bride of Demise

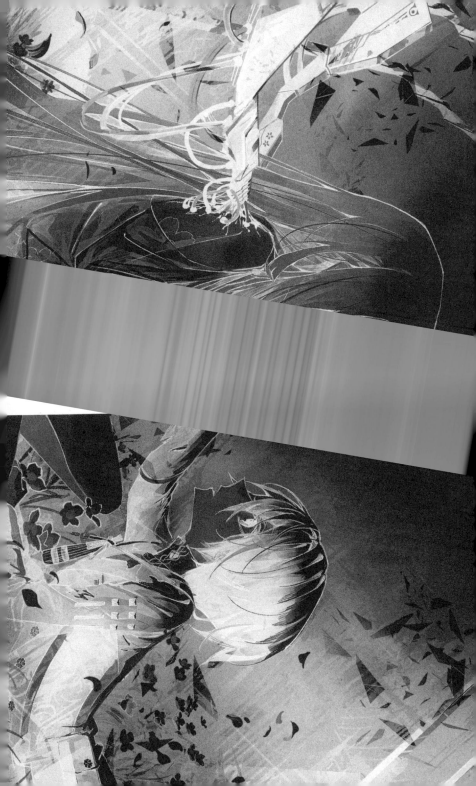

He re...
between components on the ...
sure how he'd even entered the room. The walls flashed
intervals. Looking closely, Kou noticed the flashing was in time with his heartbeat. That wasn't something achievable with current magic technology.

But it was also different from a prehistoric relic.

This space was narrow, but it extended ahead as far as he could see.

In the center stood Kagura.

He fluttered the hem of his coat and said in an easygoing manner, "Pretty sure you heard me say it. 'You can come with us and watch hell burn for what feels like an eternity' and all that... You agreed to it, remember? Can't have you giving up this quickly."

"What the hell are you talking about...? And where...?"

Kou was about to ask where they were, but he held his tongue. He had a feeling he knew what this place was. At the same moment, all sorts of little things that had felt out of place at the time came back into his mind. Heretofore meaningless pieces began to click into place.

Kou thought back.

"Okay... I'll remember for next time."

"So how're your memories? Do you remember?"

"So you're unaware?"

Kagura had said a lot of things that implied a potential "other."

Kou looked up at Kagura again.

He was a slender man with white hair, one blue eye, and one black. That color combination must be fairly rare in nature. He could swear he'd seen that man's face somewhere. At the same time, it didn't match any he'd ever seen.

Kou finally realized who those features resembled.

His hair and right eye had the same coloring as White Princess's. And his left eye was the same as Millennium Black Princess's.

As he noticed the resemblance to White Princess and Black Princess, he realized something else. If you took away his creepy expression and the differing colors, he would look a lot like Kou Kaguro.

Kou's thoughts instinctively turned to something Kagura had said.

"I lost my Bride. Well, more accurately, I consumed her."

"Actually, two. I consumed two Brides."

When Kagura used his power, masses of black feathers danced around him. If he did too much, it would "shift the world out of phase." He finally understood why.

"You... You can't be..."

"Yep, I'm one version of you. I'm the Kou Kaguro who, after spending forever trying to figure out a way forward, ended up consuming both White Princess and Black Princess and taking both their powers... And I kept trying, unable to succeed, until I was rejected by my own timeline," said Kagura coldly. He was telling the truth.

Kou stared in amazement. The man in front of him was none other than his own self, after he'd lost everything.

Kagura—the other Kou—took a step toward him.

Like he had once before, Kagura looked at Kou as if he were a dead insect. Maintaining that gaze, this man who had lost everything began to speak.

"'Enough.' That's what you thought, isn't it? That's why you're here, in this space just for my consciousness. It's based on the confinement room but not locked to any specific time. Only you can hide yourself here."

Kagura spread his arms, and Kou nodded in understanding. A pure-white space separated from time was the perfect escape. But someone else besides Kou was able to come here.

"So I'm going to say this… You haven't done anything. Do you plan to become me? Do you plan to continue living like a dead person, just stumbling through time?" asked Kagura.

"But I'm… I'm just tired. I'm tired…so tired."

"Stop screwing around; you haven't saved anything. What have you done? What have you accomplished?"

now, everything would be pointless, Kagura told him

emotion as he spoke, his fury

Some maniac who murders

In that moment, Kagura's face didn't look like expression was that of a teacher, the very last path he had chosen for himself.

Dumbstruck, Kou asked, "…S-students?"

"Yep. You're my student. A member of my precious Pandemonium. Though, at the moment, I'd really like to punch you. A teacher's always his student's ally. He has to be." Changing tack, his tone turned calm. He sounded like he was giving a confession as he said, "I'm no longer able to accomplish anything. That's why, at the end of the day, I chose to be a teacher. I wanted to give just a little bit of potential to the Pandemonium that I loved so much. And to you, too, of course."

Kagura spoke as a teacher, as someone who cared for Pandemonium.

He held a finger in front of his face and whispered like he was telling a secret, "I'll give you another little hint…a piece of confidential information that only I know."

Kagura looked at Kou with a serious expression.

He whispered, as if he were shining a single, tiny ray of light for Kou. To point him in the right direction.

"There's one place you've never gone back to, one place in your life. There are sure to be answers there. I can't go back to that place...but you can. However, it'll be painful for you to see it directly. I don't know if it'll go well. That's why you have a choice."

Kagura spread his hands. Black feathers covered him, and he chose his words with great emphasis.

Directing his voice at Kou, Kagura made an earnest offer.

"I want you to choose. I will use my power to help you, just a little. Only you will escape from the Gloaming. To be precise, you need only go back before it began. I'll make it so only you don't have to go. I'll make it so you can escape, without facing the crime of being a deserter. Other students would die immediately, but with your current powers, you should be able to live on the outside. If the current path is too painful for you, then you can take this option instead. Besides, you can't save anyone by holing yourself up, so it's the same either way, don't you think? Horrible things might keep on happening forever, after all. Or..."

He smiled; Kou was reflected in his eyes. The man's expression was astonishing; he was genuinely telling the truth. He likely could make sure Kou, alone, escaped.

Kagura nodded. For some reason, he sounded incredibly bored as he continued.

"Or you can choose the path I spoke of and watch hell burn for what feels like an eternity."

The man calmly presented the options to Kou.

His empty eyes were piercing.

Kou clenched his fists. Every despair Kou had witnessed, time and time again until now, came rushing back to him.

But he raised his head. He shook off his hesitation and replied:

"Of course I'll go back. As long as there's a way."

*   *   *

Kagura smiled with pure joy. He meaninglessly waved his fingers through the air, and a door appeared in the wall as if it had always been there.

His voice resonated as he said, "I was rejected by this timeline. I no longer have the ability to go back. You made that door. Go—and never regret a thing."

Kou bowed deeply. As he raised his head, he pushed aside his reluctance and ran.

And just like that proud moment so long ago, Kagura uttered those childlike words to Kou's back as he left.

"Good luck."

He now knew the reason for all that.

...Ah...

Kou Kaguro's current physical body was five years old. He was strapped to a metal chair. Masses of cables ran across the floor around him. A man and a woman in white paced hurriedly back and forth.

They were Kou's parents.

Kou was without any memories of his early childhood. Every time he tried thinking back to that time in his life, he was assailed by a severe headache. It was possible he was subconsciously refusing to remember because the death of his parents had been so horrifying. Once he'd come to that conclusion, he gave up and stopped trying.

Actually, that was all a lie he told himself.

He'd simply sealed those memories under a tight lid. His circumstances had been so wretched that he'd had to remove all reference to them from his mind.

His parents were Coexisters. The Coexisters' primary ideology was the desire to live in peace with the kihei. To that purpose, his parents had even laid their hands on documents imperial institutions had completely disavowed.

At one point, Kagura had said something about this.

"The even higher higher-ups apparently have some records about her. Other than some disturbing myths, though, the real details are locked behind a release key, so no one knows what's in them."

His parents took all of what those records said very seriously. Even those that were no more than delusional ravings, written in prehistory by people obsessed with the apocalypse. And they took seriously the account of the seventh Princess as "a god to end all war."

Kou's parents analyzed the Princess Series' seventh member as much as they possibly could. They believed there was still a possibility of success, that her function might yet be activated. To that end, they used the organic components from kihei to make modifications to their own son. They illicitly obtained top-secret information on the other Princess Series members and used that information to make their child into a supplemental device to the seventh Princess. They tampered with his body as far as science would allow, altering it extensively.

Simply put, Kou was no longer human.

He was a supplemental part for a kihei.

He had been "developed" to be an additional part for the seventh Princess.

That's why his emotions were so weak in the beginning.

His blood, organs, and outward appearance were very close to a human's, but more than half his body had been replaced with organic components from kihei. That allowed him to fulfill his original role of rousing White Princess. He had awakened her, even though she was incomplete.

In the end, when he'd given her all his flesh and blood, it activated the magic formulas that allowed her to travel back in time.

But my parents' beliefs were nothing but an ironic misinterpretation.

Curtain Call wasn't a god who would bring the end to a long period of war. She was a weapon, meant to exterminate everything.

Officials in the imperial capital discovered his parents' research, and considering the brutality of their experiments, they were executed. Kou was taken into protection as a child victim of human experimentation. Eventually, he was sent to the Academy, saving his life.

All his memories of these horrific experiences came rushing back to Kou. A single tear rolled down his cheek. And yet he recognized an opportunity here.

This was the only chance he would have to "remake" his body. And he already had the key he needed to make that happen.

He fought to stretch his fingers. Fortunately, he was able to grab a pen that had fallen nearby and use it to write down a certain piece of information on a table within reach.

As a result of repeating his days as a student over and over, he was now ~~able to write~~ prehistoric characters. In addition, he had memo-~~rized~~ were in the birdcage and come ~~the panels.~~

With ~~time~~ the real details of the seventh ~~Princess.~~

Kou's father showed a strong reaction when he ~~learned~~ from his son.

Though written in prehistoric characters, the author was a five-year-old child. There was a chance they would ignore it. If that happened, Kou had been prepared to wait until he grew older and tell them again before they were killed.

But his parents discussed the matter and decided to conduct a new experiment on him.

They now knew the danger of the seventh Princess as a weapon of extermination. She was a threat that people like them, who supported peace, should rightly fear. At the same time, the ability to freely manipulate time was a tempting tool for attaining their goal.

That's why his parents began to seek out a new function for Kou. A function to suppress the seventh Princess, if she were to go berserk, while maintaining Kou's capabilities to support her. With this, Kou felt sure they would continue their project.

They would further alter Kou, making him into a component for White Princess meant specifically to prevent her from rampaging.

After fifteen thousand attempts, Kou Kaguro even ended up transforming his own body.

And so he returned to the fated time.

* * *

Kou quietly looked at Millennium Black Princess.

He was at that fated day.

The final scene of the Gloaming.

The only likeness that remained was her skin, white like snow. But because they were connected, he could tell. There was no doubt that she was also White Princess. She was none other than the person he cared for most, at the end of a brutal transformation.

The current White Princess simply looked distressed. With a glance, Kou urged her to go heal Hikami. He turned back to Black Princess.

"Finally, I made it here… It took a long time, but I'm here, White Princess," he said to Black Princess.

"Boy…no, Kou… I can't, I can't… You weren't supposed to notice. I have to be Millennium Black Princess. I have to be killed here. If I'm not, fate won't change… I…"

Black Princess took an unsteady step back. A jet-black tear, mixed with altered magic, ran down her cheek.

She cried, covering her face. Shaking her head, she desperately continued her words.

"…The Gloaming happens when the king or queen of the kihei gathers so much magic that they go berserk. I took over the role of queen and withheld the magic rampaging inside me so you could have a chance at victory. I've managed to hold on to myself…but it was impossible for me to create a vessel that could hold out any longer. Soon…I will…"

"It's okay, White Princess; it'll be okay."

"I'll kill you all!" she screamed.

A massive amount of magic shot through her body. Instantly, her wings enlarged. Their jutting branches filled the air like a cosmic tree. Despair itself grew at a terrifying rate.

Every single thing was consumed, then eroded.

It was all penetrated by jet-black darkness the color of ink.

With seconds to spare, Kou grabbed the branches. Blood burst from his hands, but he didn't care.

Kou stepped farther into the fold of Black Princess's wings, into death itself.

"Kou, what are you doing?"

"Stop it; you don't need to die!"

"Come back, Kou!"

"...on?!"

"...of yourself!"

He wasn't afraid. He was...

He simply wondered whether he would be...

something.

He heard White Princess screaming from behind. Mirei, Hikami, Tsubaki, Yaguruma, and even Sasanoe were all speaking to him. He listened to their voices, all the while with a powerful thought.

...I love you.

Everything he'd lost up until this point, everything he'd neglected up until this point.

Kou Kaguro loved it all.

He reached his hands into the magic coursing through Millennium Black Princess.

The tips of his fingers burst, but he ignored it. Through intense pain, he activated his support function to its fullest capacity. Now that he had been remade, he had the ability. But he wasn't sure if it would work. His other concern was whether this counted as a significant change to the world. Though, all he was doing was using a function set in place by someone else.

He just had to hope it wouldn't shift the world out of phase.

Prepared to destroy himself if need be, Kou pushed himself past his limits.

And he completely absorbed half the magic flowing through the queen. He took it into himself and used his support function to store it all.

"…This is the end."

Afterward, silence rushed back. His vision was restored.

In front of him was Black Princess's face.

The queen's rampage had quieted, like it had never happened. Her wings shrank, the black returning to their previous feathery shape.

She stared at Kou in shock.

In her eyes, Kou saw his reflection.

He'd finally made it.

Tears streamed down his face as he took her hand. He pressed his lips to her fingers.

"Let me say it again. I give you my trust, my adoration, my fate. This I swear: I will protect you for your sake."

Kou Kaguro then smiled at the two White Princesses.

"I've kept my promise, White Princess."

The queen's rampage had abated. The kihei in the area retained their usual hostility but lost their frenzied fervor. The air seemed different. The warped flow of time that had filled the world shifted without a sound.

In that moment, the Gloaming had come to an end.

White Princess rushed to finish healing Hikami, then stood up and ran over to Kou.

"Kou!"

"Come to me, White Princess!"

She leaped from the ground, and Kou caught her head-on, wrapping his arms around her.

Her mechanical wings swayed in the air.

He'd repeated this battle so many times before, but he never once noticed that there were flowers blooming on the ground.

The surrounding vegetation was slashed and torn. Millions of petals fluttered about.

Clang-clang, the clock rang.
Ding-dong, the clock rang.
Bong-bong, the clock rang.

Kou Kaguro embraced his beloved and knew:
Just as time begins, it will one day end.
Sometime, surely.

"Wh-what the heck happened?"

"I don't know… But I can tell that something's changed!"

"Kou? Did you do something, you idiot?!"

"Did we actually…survive the Gloaming?"

"The battle's over…?"

Hikami, Mirei, Tsubaki, Yaguruma, and Sasanoe all stood.

Together, they ran over to Kou, White Princess, and Black Princess. After a moment's delay, they began cheering.

And so, on the fifteen thousandth attempt, Kou Kaguro and Pandemonium escaped the Gloaming alive, for the first time.

Academy's history.

Kou Kaguro and the others returned to the school with that achievement.

"Ah, welcome back. No report needed," said Kagura with a hand raised as they entered the classroom.

Kou looked closely at Kagura's questionable appearance. He was sitting on top of the lectern, kicking his feet like nothing had happened.

After a moment, Kou faced him and gave another deep bow.

Tsubaki, who had come with Kou, leaped from behind him and said with a pout, "What's this? Does Kagura have something on you, Kou?"

"…Something like that," he replied.

"That's a horrible thing to say! Didn't I say I'm your biggest ally?!" bragged Kagura as he fluttered the hem of his coat.

Hikami, Mirei, and Yaguruma all looked at each other at the same time. Before they could open their mouths, Sasanoe uttered a single word: "Creepy."

"Not you, tooooo. You know, you can take off that crow mask once in a while. We're all friends here, right?" said Kagura as he tapped on his own face. Sasanoe shrugged.

Kagura jumped lightly down from the lectern and looked around him.

Every member of Pandemonium was injured. Not all of them had returned. A few of them were dead.

Kagura cut through the lingering atmosphere with a clap of his hands. To everyone, he said, "Those of you who need real medical attention, head to the Department of Medicine. Good work, everyone, you made it through."

"Of course."

"What else would you expect?"

"We're Pandemonium."

"To be honest, I don't really know what happened at the end there."

The students spoke one after another. Then each of them began to move. Mirei took Hikami to the Department of Medicine, just to be on the safe side. Tsubaki fell asleep on Doll's Guardian's shoulder, totally worn out. Yaguruma sat at his desk and laid his head down. And Sasanoe made the rounds, checking on everyone else.

While that happened, Kagura moved closer to Kou. Lowering his voice, he whispered, "What about Millennium Black Princess?"

"She became my new Bride...but I thought it was too early to bring her to the Academy... She's staying in the ruins for now."

"I see... And you still have the power to move through time. You and your Brides are unstoppable now... But I do have one unfortunate piece of news."

Kagura waved a hand, then held a finger in front of his face and whispered like he was telling a secret, "You remember what I said back in the white room? That horrible things might keep on happening forever'? ...It's about that."

He suddenly narrowed his eyes and glared into the empty distance.

Almost as if he were challenging something invisible before him, Kagura said, "It's about what causes the Gloaming."

The terrifying kihei rampage that would have destroyed Pandemonium. Then an ominous prediction tumbled from his lips.

"I think there's a possibility a human might be behind it."

Those words spoke of new battles—and new enemies.

AFTERWORD

This is coming somewhat ~~~~ ~~
haven't read any of my previous work. I'm Keishi Ayasato.

I was uneasy when I first started this volume, since it's my first story taking place in a school setting, and there are a lot of unknowns. Even so, I remember that the writing went by really quickly once I actually got down to it. It was very fun to write Kou and the other members of Pandemonium.

I hope you enjoyed the relationships between Bride and Groom, and the Academy, with some pleasant moments and some moments stained with blood and battle.

Most of all, I hope you choose to continue reading the following installments.

Now then, on to my customary gratitude corner.
Thank you so much, murakaruki, for your many character designs, beautiful illustrations, and promotional manga. I cannot thank you

enough for bringing the characters to life. A huge thank you to the project managers, I and O, who I caused much grief for, and to my dear family, particularly my sister. Thank you to all the designers and people involved with publishing.

Most importantly, I would like to thank you, the readers, from the bottom of my heart. Thank you for reading about Kou and Pandemonium's first battle.

So they made it out of the Gloaming alive.
But now a new battle is set to begin.
Can you believe the second volume is planned to be published on September 25? I've already written the story. What will happen to Kou, White Princess, and the students of Pandemonium? It will make me so happy if you continue to follow their adventures.

I hope we meet again soon.

Keishi Ayasato

"Unfair.

I'm alone.

I'm always alone

all all all All

all alone!"